Jack Vance

Bad Ronald

Jack Vance

Bad Ronald

John H. Vance

Spatterlight Press Signature Series, Volume 19

Published by Spatterlight Press

Cover art by Howard Kistler

ISBN 978-1-61947-140-5

Spatterlight Press LLC

Spatterlight
P R E S S
340 S. Lemon Ave #1916
Walnut, CA 91789

www.jackvance.com

Jack Vance

Bad Ronald

CHAPTER I

ELAINE WILBY SELDOM COOKED elaborate meals; after eight hours behind a desk she felt no inclination for further toil in the kitchen, especially since she herself wasn't all that interested in food. It seemed ridiculous to invest two or three hours in some fancy concoction which tasted no better than a nice meat-loaf, and which was chewed, swallowed and digested by precisely the same processes. Ronald was not particularly fussy either, so long as he was allowed seconds and a nice dessert. Her former husband had been rather vulgar about food. He enjoyed dishes like pigs' feet with sauerkraut, and smelly cheeses, not to mention whiskey and beer, and cigars which permeated the house with the odor of dirty feet. A wonder the marriage had lasted as long as it did. Mrs. Wilby had been concerned principally for Ronald; a growing boy needed the guidance of his father, or so she had then believed. Now she knew better. Ronald was doing very well with no interference whatever from his father, and this was precisely the way Mrs. Wilby wanted it.

Tonight she had prepared a particularly nice Sunday dinner — a small rolled roast with peas and mashed potatoes, and for dessert the frozen banana-cream pie which Ronald liked so much. As Mrs. Wilby carved the roast, she reflected that this was a job Ronald should take over; carving was a skill which every gentleman should master. Of course Ronald was only sixteen, going on seventeen, and why push maturity upon the boy? He was growing up fast enough already, far too fast, in fact, for Mrs. Wilby's taste.

She watched him as he ate. Ronald had turned out well. His grades at school were better than average, and could be much improved if he'd only buckle down to his studies. A nice-looking boy, she thought, not handsome in the ordinary sense, but dignified and sensitive-looking. He could afford to lose fifteen or twenty pounds, but this was no cause for concern. Ronald had matured tardily; sooner or later he would convert all that baby fat to solid muscle. Ronald's hair was dark like his father's, and he had inherited his father's frame: heavy hips, shoulders perhaps a trifle too narrow, long legs and arms. The broad brow, the long straight nose, the full lips came straight from Elaine's side of the family, the Daskins, as did Ronald's courtesy, thoughtfulness and candor. Ronald shared her detestation of whiskey and cigars and had promised never to drink or smoke.

The thought excited a chain of recollections and she smiled grimly. Her subconscious must have been at work when she planned so festive a meal. She asked, "Do you know what day today is?"

"Of course. It's Sunday."

"What else?"

Ronald pursed his lips as he had seen his mother do. "It's not my birthday...That's next Saturday...March twentieth is your birthday...I don't think it's a holiday...I give up."

"You wouldn't remember. Ten years ago today your father and I decided to go our separate ways."

"Ten whole years! Do you miss him?"

"Not in the least."

"I don't either. But I wonder why he never comes to see us."

Ten years ago Mrs. Wilby had offered to waive child-support on condition that Armand Wilby give up part-time custody and visiting privileges, a proposition to which Armand, with his slick salesman's facility and eye for the main chance, had quickly agreed; and why trouble Ronald now with the sordid details? "He's probably just not interested," said Mrs. Wilby.

Ronald gave his head a shake of deprecation. "Well — I'm glad he lets us live in this house, even if it is an old monstrosity."

"The house is Victorian," said Mrs. Wilby evenly. "It's not a monstrosity, as you put it."

"That's what the kids at school call it."

"They don't know any better."

"I'll agree to that. They're a pretty common bunch. It's still nice of him, though."

Mrs. Wilby sniffed. Perhaps, after all, certain realities should be made clear to Ronald. "The situation isn't all that simple."

"Oh? Why not?"

"When a husband and wife are divorced," explained Mrs. Wilby, "the wife is entitled to a monthly payment called alimony, for all the trouble she's been subjected to. Instead of alimony, we are given the free use of this house."

Ronald gave an urbane nod. All was now clear. Remarkable, none-theless, how anyone—Armand Wilby, the President of the United States, Jesus Christ himself—would dare cause his mother trouble of such magnitude! Elaine Wilby, a solid well-fleshed woman with a bun of ash-blonde hair, a pale complexion and cool blue eyes, was not a woman to be trifled with. At Central Valley Hardware, where she worked an accounting machine, her decisiveness had generated a whole cycle of office legends, and even Mr. Lang accorded her an uneasy deference.

Mrs. Wilby's great hope for Ronald was a medical career. Often she envisioned him proud and tall in a white coat performing miraculous cures. Ronald Wilby, M.D.! But whenever she mused along these lines a second thought clutched at her heart. In two short years Ronald would be going off to college, followed by medical school and intern-ship. Every bit of fluff in sight would have her hooks out for him; no doubt he'd marry and start a life of his own, and what then for her? Going to work early and coming home late to a lonely old house, with only the television for company.

Ronald was aware of his mother's preoccupation. Sometimes when she refused him an extra helping of ice cream he would say, "I'm lucky to have you worrying about me. I don't know how I'll manage when I'm off on my own." Whereupon Mrs. Wilby would say, "Well, I suppose it won't matter this once. But we've really got to put you on a firm diet."

"Heavens, Mother! I'm not fat! Just big!"

"You could easily lose twenty pounds, dear. It's not a healthy con-dition."

Ronald's bulk also attracted the attention of the football coach who wanted Ronald to try out for the team; Ronald said he'd think about it. He had no taste for hard knocks, and his mother would not care for the idea, he was certain. In matters regarding his health she took no chances. A sneeze meant hot-water bottles and layers of warm clothing; every scratch was bathed in alcohol, anointed with salve and dressed in an impressive bandage. Sports were vulgar, pointless and dangerous; how could people waste money at a football game when there was so much misery and devastation in the world crying out for attention? Ronald had come to share this point of view. Still, he could see that athletes enjoyed some very real advantages. There was a certain Laurel Hansen, for instance, who doted both on football and football players, but who evaded all Ronald's advances. Would she go to the movies? Sorry, she'd been asked to a slumber party. Would she like to drop by the House of Music to help pick out some records? Sorry, she had to wash her hair. What about Henry's Joint after school for a sundae? Sorry, she had a tennis date.

The situation gnawed at Ronald's self-esteem, even though he could readily perceive the intellectual limitations of such prognathous young louts as Jim Neale and Ervin Loder, both on good terms with Laurel Hansen. Ronald himself, of course, was a natural aristocrat, a gallant figure after the Byronic tradition, driven by a wild and tempestuous imagination. He had written several poems, among them *Ode to Dawn*, *The Gardens of My Mind*, *The World's an Illusion*, all of which his mother considered excellent. When he looked in the mirror and held his head just right, the heaviness at his cheeks and jaw fell away, and there, gazing back through heavy-lidded eyes, stood a dashing cavalier with a long noble nose and a dreamer's forehead, whom no girl could conceivably resist. If only he could induce Laurel off somewhere alone and enchant her with the splendor of his visions! For Ronald, a devotee of fantasy fiction, had contrived a wonderful land which lay behind the Mountain of the Seven Ghouls and across the Acriline Sea: Atranta. Ronald had spoken of Atranta and its inhabitants to his mother, but she seemed rather skeptical. On second thought, perhaps it was best not to confide in Laurel, not for a while anyway; he didn't want her thinking him a weirdo.

CHAPTER II

ON RONALD'S BIRTHDAY Mrs. Wilby always prepared a special dinner of Ronald's favorite dishes. This year the process would be less hectic than usual, since Ronald's seventeenth birthday fell on Saturday. For months Ronald had dreamed of impossible gifts: a motorcycle, a small color TV for his room, a three-day tour to Disneyland, a high-power telescope, a sailing kayak and also — this with a lewd private snicker — Laurel Hansen's underpants. He had dropped hints in regard to the motorcycle, to which his mother gave short shrift: motorcycles were simply invitations to injury, and the people who rode them were a seedy group indeed, and what was wrong with Ronald's fine three-speed bicycle of which he had been so proud only a few years before?

"Nothing's wrong with the bike," Ronald growled. "It's just that I'm old enough to drive; in fact I've been old enough for a whole year. I don't suppose you'd let me get a car."

"You suppose correctly. One car in the family is enough. Can you imagine what the insurance would cost?"

"Probably a lot."

Mrs. Wilby nodded curtly. "Still, it's time you learned to drive, just in case of emergencies. But put the extravagant notions about cars and motorcycles out of your head. A car would interfere with your grades, which aren't all that good for a person who intends to go on to university and medical school."

Ronald gave a disconsolate shrug. "Just as you say."

Saturday morning arrived, and Ronald found himself moderately pleased with his gifts. There was the stylish new 'Safari' jacket he had coveted; several books: *Lives of the Great Composers, How to Construct Your*

Own Telescope, Is There Life on Other Worlds? by Poul Anderson, and the Tolkien *Lord of the Rings* trilogy. A greeting card from Aunt Margaret in Pennsylvania was given substance by the attached five-dollar bill; there was also a wallet of simulated alligator skin, with a certificate entitling Ronald Arden Wilby to ten lessons at the Delta Driving School. Ronald reflected that things might have gone far worse. The jacket fit perfectly; inspecting himself in the mirror Ronald thought that he cut quite a fine figure, and his mother agreed. "The color is very good on you, and the jacket is cut well: you really look quite trim."

Breakfast went according to Ronald's dictates: pineapple juice, Danish pastry with hot chocolate, followed by pork sausages and strawberry waffles with whipped cream. As Ronald ate he looked through his books. The *Lives of the Great Composers* he recognized as an attempt to interest him in 'good music', as distinguished from the 'din and rumpus' to which Ronald usually listened. For a fact, the book looked interesting, and he saw some rather rare episodes in the early life of Mozart which his mother certainly had not noticed.

He took up *How to Construct Your Own Telescope*. "Hmm," said Ronald, "this is interesting!... I didn't know that... They say grinding a mirror entails a great deal of painstaking work!"

"Nothing really worthwhile comes easy," said Mrs. Wilby.

"I'd just as soon work with a set of lenses," said Ronald. "They come in kits from Edmund Scientific, and there wouldn't be all that rubbing and polishing."

Mrs. Wilby made no further comment. Astronomy, whether by lens or by mirror, would make a wonderful hobby for Ronald, who spent far too much time daydreaming over heaven-knows-what. She cleared the table while Ronald considered the advantages of a telescope. His bedroom window commanded a view of the Murray house, about a hundred yards distant. One of the second-story windows opened into the bedroom of the Murray twins, Della and Sharon, and it might be interesting to see what transpired there of evenings. A really powerful telescope might resolve significant details even at the distance of Laurel Hansen's house, six blocks away. Unfortunately, a stand of eucalyptus trees obscured the view. Might it be possible to climb a eucalyptus tree carrying a telescope?... Something to think about, at any rate.

At three o'clock Mrs. Wilby served a birthday dinner of chicken-fried steak, mashed potatoes, and a big banana-cream cake from the bakery. Ronald extinguished the candles with a single blast, and elected to accompany his cake with a helping of vanilla ice cream.

After dinner Ronald wondered what Laurel might be up to and sauntered to the telephone. He started to dial, then hesitated. If he simply paid Laurel a visit, she wouldn't have a chance to say no. He'd be able to talk with her, and perhaps she'd recognize the glamour and scope of his personality, and who knows what might come of the episode?

He went to his room, combed his hair, sprayed himself with *Tahitian Prince* cologne. He donned his new 'Safari' jacket, glanced in the mirror, and gave the image a jaunty salute. He went downstairs. "I'm going out for a walk," he told his mother. "I'll be back after a bit."

Ronald marched along at a good pace, sternly erect, the better to set off his jacket. From Orchard Street he turned into Honeysuckle Lane, which skirted the rear of the old Hastings estate, walked down to Drury Way, turned right, and walked another two blocks to Laurel Hansen's home. Ralph Hansen, Laurel's father, operated the Sierra Lumber Company; the Hansens, by Oakmead standards, lived luxuriously in a large ranch-style house with a façade of used brick. White shutters flanked the windows; the shake roof was stained green. Mrs. Hansen was prominent in Oakmead society and also an assiduous gardener. Rose bushes lined the walk; chrysanthemums, asters, daisies and petunias bloomed around the edges of an immaculate lawn.

Ronald sauntered up the path, annoyed to find his heart beating faster than usual. There was no reason for nervousness, so he assured himself, none whatever. At the front door he settled his jacket, rang the bell, and waited. Perhaps Laurel was home alone; she'd look forth, wistful and lonely, and there would be Ronald. So many wonderful things might happen…Laurel's mother opened the door — a slim, handsome woman of forty with a modish thatch of shining silver hair, sea-blue eyes like Laurel's, features delicate and brittle as porcelain. She had never met Ronald and looked him blankly up and down. "Yes?"

Ronald cleared his throat and spoke in his best voice. "Is Laurel home?"

Mrs. Hansen failed to notice Ronald's suave courtesy. "She's out in back."

"I wonder if I might see her."

Mrs. Hansen made an indifferent gesture. "Go right on through. You'll find her out at the pool."

Ronald marched stiffly into the house, where he paused, intending to chat a moment or two, but Mrs. Hansen had already gone off down the hall. A chilly woman, and rather proud of herself, thought Ronald. He looked around the room: Laurel's native habitat. The intimacy was thrilling. She breathed this air, she sat in these chairs, she looked at these pictures, she warmed herself at this fireplace! Ronald took a deep breath and expanded his soul, trying to absorb the environment: he felt he knew Laurel better already.

He heard light steps; Mrs. Hansen came back into the room with eyebrows slightly raised. She spoke in a bright clear voice, "Laurel's out in back."

"Oh yes," said Ronald hastily. "I was just admiring the room."

Mrs. Hansen seemed not to hear. "This way." She led Ronald across the living room, through a pair of sliding doors, and out upon the patio. "Laurel!" called Mrs. Hansen. "Someone to see you."

Laurel, splashing in the swimming pool with her friends, paid no heed.

Mrs. Hansen said to Ronald, "I imagine you can get her attention one way or another."

"Thank you very much," said Ronald. He advanced upon the pool. The situation was not at all to his liking; he felt hurt and angry with Laurel. She should have been home alone, moping and mournful, waiting for him to call. Instead, look at her: callously enjoying herself with her friends. There were two girls, Wanda McPherson and Nancy Rucker; and two boys: Jim Neale, fullback on the football team, and Martin Woolley. Jim Neale's father owned Oakmead Liquors, which should have blasted Jim's social status: yet here he swam in the Hansen pool with complete aplomb! Not only that, Laurel was climbing up his back and diving from his shoulders, to Ronald's disgust and disapproval. Martin Woolley, the senior class president, lacked Jim Neale's physique; in fact, he seemed all arms, legs and ribs. His hair was a nondescript tangle; his nose hung like an icicle; his mouth drooped in a saturnine leer. Martin's popularity was a complete puzzle to Ronald, but there he sprawled beside the swimming pool with Wanda and Nancy hanging on his every word.

Ronald went to stand beside the pool. "Hello everybody."

Wanda, Nancy and Martin acknowledged his presence politely enough; Laurel gave her hand a casual flip; Jim, wallowing down in the water, ignored him. Ronald watched as he swam underwater, seized Laurel's ankles, put his head between her legs, raised up and tossed her screaming backwards into the water. Laurel wore a white bikini; Ronald watched in fascination as she paddled to the ladder and climbed out to stand dripping. Laurel was a blonde elf: slender, flawless, exquisite, enticing as a bowl of strawberries and ice cream. Never had Ronald seen anything so urgently beautiful. But how could her mother allow it? The bikini concealed nothing! She might as well have been nude!

Ronald sauntered around the pool. Laurel glanced at him sidewise and spoke in a voice almost without inflection. "Well, Ronald, how are you today?"

"Oh, fine. I was just wandering around and I thought I'd drop by and see what you were doing."

"I've been swimming."

"I see." Ronald hesitated, then asked, "Are you busy tonight? I mean, would you like to go to a show?"

Laurel shook her head. "I'm doing something else."

Ronald thrust his hands in his pockets and frowned out over the pool. "Well — what about tomorrow night?"

"We're having company."

"Oh…Well, maybe some other time."

Laurel said nothing. Jim Neale came floating past on his back; Laurel stepped forward, put her foot on his chest, and pushed him under. "That's for ducking me! Now we're even!"

Jim splashed up some water, and Ronald jumped back in indignation. "Hey! I'm up here too!"

"It's just water," said Jim. "It'll evaporate in an hour or so."

"Some people even drink it," said Martin.

Ronald forced an easy smile. "I don't object to water, but I'd just as soon it evaporated someplace else."

Laurel went to the diving board, poised herself, and dived. Ronald went to a deck chair and sat down, an elegant sophisticate amused by the happy play of children. He couldn't take his eyes off Laurel. The little patches of white cloth were more explicit than nothing whatever!

Ronald sat half an hour, no one paying him any attention. Mrs. Hansen came out to the pool. "Mrs. Rucker just called. They're starting up the charcoal. You'd better step lively if you want any steak."

The group went chattering off to the dressing rooms. Ronald remained in the deck chair.

He sat a half-minute. Then he rose to his feet and walked around the house, through a gate, and out upon the street.

Head lowered, shoulders hunched, he strode back up Drury Way. After a block he halted to gaze back toward the Hansen house. If emotion could be projected in a beam, if hate could be made hot, the house would roil up in a burst of flame, and all within would come dancing out, to roll and tumble across the lawn. Let them all die, the worthless futile creatures! He'd save none of them. Except Laurel. He'd take her to a far island, or a snowbound cabin, with nobody there but the two of them! How she'd regret her conduct! How she'd plead for forgiveness! He'd say, "Remember at your swimming party, how you went away and left me alone by the pool? I don't forget things like that!"

Unfortunately, such a requital was difficult to arrange.

Breathing hard through his nose, Ronald continued up Drury Way, with sunset light shining through the poplar trees of the Hastings estate. At Honeysuckle Lane he glanced back once more and saw the group come forth and climb into Jim Neale's old Volkswagen. Ronald grimaced. He should have flattened the tires, or pulled a wire out of the distributor. Except that Jim Neale would guess the culprit's identity and that wouldn't be good.

After the barbecue Jim would no doubt take Laurel off in his car. Jim was bold; Laurel was feckless; Ronald knew what was going to happen. He felt curiously sick; his throat throbbed with woe and rage and mortification. No help for it, but sometime, somehow, he would get his own back!

He turned up Honeysuckle Lane, and the setting sun at his back projected a gigantic shadow ahead, which for fifty yards or so provided

Ronald a gloomy diversion. How grotesquely the shadow reacted to his movements!

Toward him came Carol Mathews, riding her bicycle. Carol, eleven years old, as blonde as Laurel Hansen, lived around the corner on May Street. The sun shone into her face, illuminating her beautiful green eyes. She failed to see Ronald and rode directly into him. Ronald caught the handlebars and backing away brought the bicycle to a halt. The bicycle fell over; Ronald caught Carol before she fell to the ground and held her against his chest. "What do you think you're doing?" Ronald snarled.

"I'm sorry!" she gasped. "I didn't see you!"

Carol was already adolescent; Ronald could feel her breasts against his chest. He began to seethe with a complicated emotion. None of these blonde girls cared what they were doing; they thought they could get away with anything! He bent his head and kissed Carol's mouth. She stared up in amazement, then tried to squirm loose. "Let me go!"

"Just a minute," said Ronald. "You've got something coming."

"No I don't! Let me go!"

"Not so fast." Ronald's hand, seemingly of its own volition, groped under her skirt. Carol yelled in outrage. Ronald clapped his hand over her mouth. He glanced up and down the lane. Empty. He growled into Carol's ear, "Are you going to yell? Are you? You'd better not!"

Carol looked up with glazed green eyes and shook her head. Ronald took away his hand, and she gasped for breath. "Please don't, please let me go! I didn't do it on purpose…"

"I'm not thinking about that now." Clamping her mouth once more, Ronald dragged her, kicking and hopping, squirming and jerking, into the grounds at the back of the old Hastings Estate. Pulling her face free, Carol gasped, "I don't want to go in here!" She started to scream; Ronald thrust his hand over the wetness of her open mouth; she bit his palm, and received a slap in stern retribution.

Carol made frantic noises through his hand: she seemed to be saying, "I can't breathe! I can't breathe!"

Ronald eased his grip. "Don't you dare yell! Do you hear? Say yes!"

Carol obstinately said nothing and tried to pull away; Ronald cuffed her and dragged her back. He inspected the overgrown old garden. Carol whimpered, "What are you going to do?"

"You'll see."

"No!" Carol raised her voice once more; Ronald instantly closed off her mouth and thrust his face down to within six inches of hers. He spoke in measured ominous tones, "You'd better not bite me again, and you'd better not yell!"

Carol stared up like a hypnotized rabbit. Ronald withdrew his hand and Carol squeezed her eyes shut, as if by this means to obliterate the entire situation. Ronald thrust her to the ground under an old weeping willow tree.

"Relax," said Ronald. "This is going to be fun. Really it is."

Carol's mouth sagged and warped; tears began to stream down her cheeks. "Please don't! No! No, no, no!"

"Be quiet! And afterwards you'd better not tell!"

Carol lay sobbing. Leaves and grass had caught in her hair; she looked disheveled and distraught. This, thought Ronald, was what Laurel would look like under similar circumstances. That would have made it even better.

Ronald now decided to be nice. He stroked her hair. "There now. That was fun, wasn't it?"

"No."

"Of course it was! Let's do it again tomorrow."

"No!"

"Why not? I'll…" Ronald raised his head and listened through the dusk. Someone was calling. "Carol! Carol!" A woman's voice.

"That's my mother! I'm going home right now!" Carol started to sit up.

Ronald pushed her back down. "Just a minute. Are you going to tell?"

Carol compressed her lips and shook her head: a shake of resentment and obstinacy rather than a commitment to silence.

"Oh come on!" Ronald spoke in a bluff cajoling voice. "Wouldn't you like to do it again, maybe tomorrow?"

"No. And you won't either, because you'll be in jail." She pulled away from him, sobbing bitterly, and scrambled to her knees.

Ronald jerked her back. "Just a minute. You've got to promise to keep this a secret."

Twisting and pushing Carol tried to break away; she opened her mouth to scream. Ronald bore her to the ground, clasped her mouth; she bit his hand and, gasping, finally managed to emit a wild yell. Ronald seized her throat. "Be quiet!" he hissed. "Be quiet! Be quiet!"

Carol fought and thrashed and kicked, and Ronald squeezed her neck till she became quiet, and when he loosened his grip she lay limp.

"Carol," said Ronald, peering down into her face. "Carol?"

A weird cold sensation came over Ronald. He spoke in an urgent voice, "Carol! Are you just fooling?...I was just fooling, too. Let's be friends." And hopefully: "If you won't tell anyone, I won't."

Carol said nothing. Her eyes, half-open, reflected glints of gray twilight; her tongue lolled from her mouth.

"She's dead," muttered Ronald. "Oh my, oh my. She's dead."

He jumped to his feet and stood staring down through the shadows. "I mustn't lose my head," said Ronald. "I've got to think."

He stood listening through the twilight. Silence, except for the far hum of town traffic. Here, under the old weeping willow, all noises were hushed.

Ronald told himself, "I am different. I have always known I am different. I am superior to the ordinary person: stronger of purpose and more intelligent. Now I must prove this. Very well! I accept the challenge of fate!" He drew a deep breath, and exhaled. His nerves must be steel, his will strong as that of some unearthly supercreature! So then: first things first. The body must be concealed. He looked around the dim old garden and walked cautiously to a shed, where he found an ancient spade. Just the thing. He selected a spot to the side of the shed and began to dig, first removing his 'Safari' jacket so as not to soil it. Hark! a car coming down Honeysuckle Lane!

A squeal of brakes. The car halted. Ronald ran to the fence and peered out into the lane.

The car was a tan and white station wagon, which Ronald half-recognized. The headlights burned through the twilight to illuminate an object in the middle of the road: Carol's bicycle. Ronald's heart jumped up to fill his throat.

The driver alighted from the car and moved into the glare of the headlights: a big rawboned man with the face of an Apache chieftain. Ronald knew him for Donald Mathews, Carol's father. Could he be out searching for Carol? More likely he was just coming home from work. For a moment he stood looking down at the bicycle, clearly vexed by what he assumed to be Carol's carelessness; then he picked up the bicycle, loaded it into the back of the station wagon, and drove off.

There was no time to waste. Ronald thrust the body into the hole and spaded dirt upon the pale glimmer. One moment! Carol's torn underpants. Into the hole and buried with the rest. Ronald stamped the loam down firm and solid, then scattered leaves and twigs and rotten palm fronds on top. He replaced the spade in the shed after wiping it clean of fingerprints, then took one of the palm fronds and worked it over the ground wherever he had walked, hoping thereby to obliterate his footprints. Now he had better leave. He jumped the fence into Honeysuckle Lane and ran with long, fleet strides up to Orchard Street. Here he paused to catch his breath and take stock of the situation. The street was clear of traffic; Ronald continued at a more sedate pace, his mind full of veering thoughts. Certain notions he rejected as unworthy of consideration. The situation was at an end. A deplorable affair — an accident, really. He had carried it off very well. No doubt he should have moved the bicycle before Mr. Mathews found it, but a person couldn't think of everything. From now on, so far as he was concerned, the episode was finished — done with, null and void, nonexistent. He would put it clear out of his mind, as if it had never happened.

He climbed the steps to the front porch and paused once more. His mother was wonderfully keen; he must act normal at all costs. Light, easy, suave, nerveless: in short, his usual self.

He entered the house. His mother sat in the living room, watching a television travelogue. "Hello, Mother," said Ronald.

"Hello, dear. Where have you been?"

"Oh — here and there. At Laurel Hansen's house, mostly. I should have taken my swimsuit; everybody else was in the pool."

"Laurel Hansen? Isn't she the little blonde girl?"

Ronald twitched his lips. He didn't like the sound of the words "the little blonde girl". Carol really wasn't all that little; in fact — but this was a line of thought he absolutely intended not to pursue, now or ever.

"You look a little flushed, dear," said Mrs. Wilby. "And what's that in your hair?"

Ronald brushed at the object. "It's just a leaf." He laughed. "I guess I got a bit sunburnt out by the pool."

"It's too bad you didn't think to take your bathing suit. But there'll be other times. Where's your new jacket? You'd better hang it neatly on a hanger so it will keep its shape…What's the trouble?"

Ronald stood stiff and still.

CHAPTER III

"THE JACKET — IT'S AT the Hansen's. I got warm and took it off...I'll run back now and get it."

"Don't bother, dear, it's dark. I'm sure it will be safe until tomorrow."

"I'd just as soon run down and get it now. There's something I want to tell Laurel."

Mrs. Wilby darted an appraising glance at Ronald. It wasn't like him to be so energetic. But he was probably worried about his lovely new jacket. She returned to the affairs of the New Guinea headhunters.

Ronald ran back down Orchard Street, the pulse thumping in his throat. He turned into Honeysuckle Lane, and stopped short at the sight of headlights and a group of men at the back of the Hastings estate. Fascinated, Ronald stole a hundred feet closer. Two of the cars were police cars. Bright lights flickered around the grounds of the Hastings estate. Mr. Mathews had acted swiftly indeed.

Ronald turned and stumbled home. He opened the door, faltered into the living room, and slumped upon the couch. Mrs. Wilby looked at him in consternation. "Why, what's the trouble? Can't you find your jacket?"

Ronald found that he could not speak. Words stuck in his throat. He lifted his arms and beat the side of his head in frustration.

Mrs. Wilby flicked off the television. "What in the world is wrong? Ronald! Don't act that way! It can't be all that bad!"

"It's worse than bad," croaked Ronald. "It's the baddest thing that could be. I don't know how to tell you."

Mrs. Wilby said in a metallic voice, "Perhaps you'd better start at the beginning."

"I was coming home from the Hansen's," said Ronald. "In the lane I met a girl — Carol Mathews. She asked me to come with her into the old Hastings place to do something for her: to help her find her dog. I went in, and, well, she acted, well, fresh. Sexy, I guess you'd say. Anyway, she wanted me to do it with her, and, well, I did. Then she said she'd tell unless I gave her some money, and I said I wouldn't. She began to yell, and I tried to stop her, and, well, we had a big fight, and by accident…Well, she was dead."

There was a long silence.

"Ronald," breathed Mrs. Wilby. "Oh Ronald, how awful. How awful."

Ronald proceeded more rapidly. "I was afraid and scared. Horrified. It was all an accident, really Mother, I didn't mean to do it, it happened so fast, I couldn't help it."

"I understand that, Ronald…But what did you do then?"

"Well, I found a shovel and buried her. And then I came home. But I left my jacket. And when I went back just now the police were there. Mr. Mathews found her bicycle in the lane and I guess he figured that's where she was."

Elaine Wilby sat back in the chair, the structure of her life tumbling into ruins about her. And Ronald's life as well. There would be no mercy for Ronald. They'd take him and lock him up among criminals and degenerates.

Ronald said in a hollow voice, "I don't know what to do…I don't want to go to jail, and leave home, and leave you…What would they do to me?"

"I've got to think," said Mrs. Wilby.

After a moment Ronald said, "Nobody saw me. I covered all my tracks. There weren't any…" His voice drifted away. He had caught the handlebars of Carol's bicycle; he might have left his fingerprints on the metal.

Mrs. Wilby wearily shook her head. "They've got the jacket. The police will trace it to Gorman's by the label, and the girl will remember that I bought it. It was the last one in stock. Oh Ronald, how could you do such a thing?"

"I don't know, Mother, I really don't. I just lost my head. If she hadn't said she'd tell and wanted money and started to yell…"

"That makes no difference with the police. It'll be in all the papers. We're simply ruined! And the wonderful career we'd planned for you."

Ronald asked uncertainly, "Do you think I should go to the police and tell how it happened?"

Mrs. Wilby closed her eyes. This was a nightmare. How could such a thing happen to her? The circumstances were unreal! Unreasonable! Unjust! She didn't deserve them, nor did poor, foolish, scared Ronald who, after all, wasn't much more than a little boy, her own little boy, who trusted her to help him and protect him. But how?

"I really don't quite know what to do," she said in a passionless voice. "I don't have the money to send you away. Your Aunt Margaret...but she wouldn't involve herself in such a mess. Your father..." Mrs. Wilby became silent; the idea was too futile to verbalize.

"It was really an accident, Mother! I wish I'd never seen her!"

"Yes, dear, I understand this very well...You won't go to jail. We've got a day or two until they trace the jacket."

"But what can we do?"

"I don't really know."

"Oh how I wish this hadn't happened," moaned Ronald. "If I could only..."

"Ronald, be quiet. I've got to think."

Five minutes passed, with Ronald sniffling and fidgeting and making gurgling sounds in his throat to indicate his remorse and despair. Mrs. Wilby sat like a stone.

At last she stirred. Ronald looked at her hopefully. She gave her head a somber shake. "It's just a terrible mess. I really don't know what to do."

"Couldn't we both go away somewhere? Maybe to the mountains, or someplace where no one would look for us?"

Mrs. Wilby sniffed. "That's quite impractical, Ronald. I don't care to live the life of a fugitive. Even more to the point, I don't have any ready money in the house."

"I could go to work and support both of us," said Ronald hollowly.

Mrs. Wilby uttered a bark of sad laughter. "Quite honestly, I don't know what to do. Nothing seems feasible. I suppose I could send you away somewhere..."

"Oh Mother! I don't want to go off alone!"

Mrs. Wilby heaved a sigh. "I know, dear. I don't want you to leave. The least objectionable scheme is to hide you somewhere until I could get some money together. Then we'd move to the east coast or perhaps Florida, and start life all over again."

"That sounds as good as anything," said Ronald, blinking back tears for the old easy happy life, forever lost and gone. "I don't mind anything, so long as they don't take me away from you."

"That won't happen, dear. I'm just wondering where we could put you."

"There's the shed out in back. I could stay there."

Mrs. Wilby shook her head. "It's the first place the police would look."

"There's the attic. Remember the den I built up there when I was little?"

"They'll search the attic, very carefully, and any other obvious place. And the attic is a very long way to bring up your meals and then carry down the chamber pot, which would be the only possible method of sanitation. We'd want some place where you could live in decency and cleanliness, which means a bathroom…There's our own downstairs bathroom, of course."

"The downstairs bathroom? That doesn't seem too practical."

"To the contrary," said Mrs. Wilby. "It's quite practical indeed." She rose to her feet. "But we've got to work very hard."

The front door to the Wilby house opened into a hall. To the left lay the living room, to the right the dining room. Directly ahead, wide stairs rose to a landing, then reversed up to the second floor. Under these stairs was the bathroom: a combination cloakroom and lavatory, with a toilet at the far end under the landing. Only three months before Mrs. Wilby and Ronald had repapered both the front hall and the bathroom, to make them brighter and less old-fashioned. Now they took the door off the hinges, pried loose the molding and the doorjamb. To the studs, the header, and across the floor they nailed cleats, hammering as quietly as they could. Into the aperture they fitted a piece of plasterboard left over from the refinishing of Ronald's room.

Before they nailed the plasterboard in place they brought a cot into the bathroom, several blankets, and an electric heater. The far wall of the bathroom adjoined the kitchen pantry. They cut away the lath and plaster of the bathroom wall, and low under the bottom shelf in the pantry sawed the plywood to make a secret little door, which Ronald used once or twice to demonstrate that he could get in and out. Then they nailed the plasterboard in place to fill the doorway, and carefully pasted wallpaper over the plasterboard.

The baseboard across the bottom of the doorway posed a problem, which they solved by prying a suitable length from an upstairs bedroom and fitting it into place.

The downstairs bathroom had now disappeared. The time was four o'clock in the morning.

Ronald from now on must not be seen. Taking a chance that Mrs. Schumacher, their rather inquisitive neighbor, was asleep at this hour, Mrs. Wilby carried the old door and the old moldings to the rubbish area behind the garage, where they made an inconspicuous addition to the material already there.

Ronald meantime brought into the lair his new birthday books, his radio with its ear-plug attachment, pajamas, bathrobe, slippers, a few other odds and ends.

Mrs. Wilby carefully cleaned the front hall and as a last refinement hung a picture across the old doorway. The illusion, in her opinion, was perfect; the lair was undetectable.

Dawn began to show gray in the east. "You'd better go in now," said Mrs. Wilby, "and remember! You must learn to be quiet! And never flush the toilet unless you're sure it's safe to do so!"

"One more thing," said Ronald rather importantly, "I want my Atranta notebooks; I might as well have something to work on. And I'm kind of hungry."

"Get your notebooks, and then go in. It's getting light outside."

Ronald brought the notebooks down from his room. "I guess that's about all I really need."

His mother hardly seemed to hear him. "From now on we just can't take any chances. Two knocks will be the danger signal! That means: no noise! Not a sound! When the coast is clear, I'll knock four times.

Now go on in so you'll be safe. I'll fix your breakfast and pass it in to you."

Ronald looked sadly around the kitchen and into the dining room where he and his mother had enjoyed so many pleasant meals. Mrs. Wilby's emotions, which she had carefully held under control, almost got the better of her. He's saying goodby to all this, she thought, and for a fact it is goodby, because things can never be the same again, for either of us!

Ronald spoke in a hushed voice: "How long do you think it will be?"

"I just don't know. But we've got to be realistic, and I would guess several months at least."

Ronald looked glumly over his shoulder toward the secret door. "Several months?"

"At least. Perhaps as long as six months. I know it's difficult, for both of us, but it can't be helped."

"I don't mind, Mother, really I don't...I just hope it won't be too long."

"I hope so, too. As soon as we have enough money, and it's safe to do so, we'll leave. Meanwhile we'll have to be patient and very, very careful. The police will be on the lookout, and we can't do anything rash. That reminds me of something I'd better do. You go on into your den."

Ronald went into the pantry, slid open the secret door, crawled into his lair, and pushed the door shut behind him. Mrs. Wilby examined the pantry to make sure that the door was both inconspicuous and secure. She bent over. "Ronald! Can you hear me?"

"Yes." Ronald's voice was somewhat muffled.

"From now on, you're hiding! Don't call or knock or make any sound unless I give you the all-clear signal."

"What about some breakfast?"

"In just a few minutes."

Mrs. Wilby went up to Ronald's room and went to the box where he kept his savings. Twenty-two dollars. She took the money and left the box on his study table. She opened several of his drawers and rummaged up the contents, and left one of the drawers half-open. She lay down on her bed, in order to disarrange the spread and dent the pillows. The bed felt so soothing and she was so bone-weary she just wanted to lie there and rest, but she forced herself to her feet. There seemed to be nothing else to do at the moment. One great relief: today was Sunday and she need not worry about work.

Returning downstairs she fixed Ronald a good breakfast of oatmeal, bacon, eggs, toast and chocolate milk, and set it on a tray. She rapped four times on the secret door, pulled it aside and slid Ronald's breakfast through into the lair.

She washed dishes, made coffee for herself and sat down at the dining room table to wait.

Chapter IV

A FEW MINUTES AFTER ten o'clock the doorbell rang. Mrs. Wilby was still sitting at the table, a cup of lukewarm coffee in front of her. She rose to her feet. Now it starts. If ever she needed to keep her wits about her, it was now. Through the dining room window she glimpsed a man in a tan whipcord jacket sauntering past and into the back yard.

With slow, almost ponderous, steps, Mrs. Wilby went into the front hall where she gave two soft but definite raps on the wall. She listened. No sound from within. She opened the front door.

Two men stood on the porch: a stocky pink-faced man in a rumpled gray-brown suit, the other a taller younger man, hazel-eyed and quite handsome, in the uniform of a deputy sheriff.

"Mrs. Wilby?" asked the older man, and Mrs. Wilby thought she had never seen eyes so gray and hard.

"Yes. What do you want?"

"We're from the Sheriff's office. I'm Sergeant Lynch." He displayed credentials. "May we come in?"

Mrs. Wilby silently drew back, and the two men entered. They walked very lightly for such strong, heavy men, she thought.

She took them into the living room and pulled back the drapes, letting light into the room. "What do you want? Is it…" the words went heavy in her mouth. Both men were watching her with calm expressions; they seemed detached rather than unsympathetic.

Lynch said, "We're here on an unpleasant errand, Mrs. Wilby. Ronald Wilby is your son?"

Mrs. Wilby nodded. She had rehearsed this scene several times. "Why do you ask?"

"Will you please call him?"

Mrs. Wilby walked to the green plush armchair and sat down. "Why are you asking these questions?" And she forced herself to ask, "What has Ronald done?"

"Late yesterday a young girl was assaulted and killed. The evidence suggests that Ronald may know something about the business. This must come as shocking news to you, but the situation is as I've explained it, and now I'll have to ask you to call Ronald. It would also be wise for you to have a lawyer present while we're questioning him."

"Ronald isn't here," said Mrs. Wilby. "He left the house last night and hasn't come home."

For ten seconds the two policemen stared at her, and Mrs. Wilby wondered if guilty knowledge might be printed on her face. The deputy spoke for the first time. "What time did he come home yesterday afternoon?"

"I don't remember exactly. It must have been about six, or perhaps a bit later."

"Did he seem disturbed? Did he mention or even hint that he might have done something wrong?"

"Not in so many words."

"What do you mean by that?"

Mrs. Wilby spoke in a weary voice. "He didn't seem himself. I asked if anything were wrong and he said no. He'd been over to a friend's house, and I thought something might have happened that he didn't want to talk about, so I didn't press him."

"What friend had he visited?"

Mrs. Wilby sat dull and passive. The deputy repeated the question.

"He went to Laurel Hansen's house, on Drury Way."

"And he was disturbed when he came home. What did he say?"

Mrs. Wilby put her hand to her forehead. After a moment she said, "I can't believe Ronald would do such a thing. It's not like him. He's always been gentle."

"I certainly sympathize with you, Mrs. Wilby," said Lynch.

"How can you be sure Ronald did this?"

"We have several items of evidence," said Lynch. "His flight certainly isn't the act of an innocent person."

Mrs. Wilby sat silent.

"Do you have any idea where he might have gone?"

"No idea whatever."

Lynch glanced at the deputy, who rose to his feet. Lynch asked, "Do you mind if we have a look around? He just might be hiding — in the attic, or in a closet, or some such place."

Mrs. Wilby gave a weary shrug. "Look as much as you like."

The two men went upstairs. Mrs. Wilby leaned back in the chair and closed her eyes, listening to the footsteps as the men examined Ronald's room, his closet, the other three bedrooms, the bathroom and the attic. Returning downstairs, they passed through the dining room into the kitchen and out upon the back porch, where Lynch spoke to the man stationed in the back yard. A moment later Mrs. Wilby heard someone open the lattice door giving into the crawl-space under the house.

Lynch and the deputy returned to the living room. "Do you feel up to answering a few questions, Mrs. Wilby? I won't trouble you any more than necessary, I promise you."

"Ask your questions," said Mrs. Wilby in a cold voice. Nothing would arouse their suspicion so much as over-friendliness.

"You're divorced from Ronald's father?"

"Yes."

"Is Ronald friendly with his father?"

"He doesn't feel much one way or the other. He'd hardly be likely to seek him out, if that's what you're after."

"Where would Ronald be likely to go? Have you any ideas?"

"No. None at all."

"Don't forget, Mrs. Wilby," the deputy inserted, "it's to everyone's advantage to get this matter cleared up as soon as possible."

"Except Ronald's." Mrs. Wilby spoke bitterly.

"If Ronald committed this act, and it appears that he did, then he's got to be restrained before he does it again. I'm sure you'll agree to this."

"Of course. But he's my son, and I'm not convinced that he did what you say he did. Who was the girl?"

"Carol Mathews. She lived on May Street. About six o'clock she started home from a friend's house on her bicycle, apparently by way of Honeysuckle Lane, behind the Hastings place. Ronald would also have come by Honeysuckle Lane on his way home from Drury Way."

"That doesn't prove anything," declared Mrs. Wilby. "It might have been anyone. Perhaps Ronald saw what was going on, perhaps the real criminal threatened him, or frightened him in some way…"

"We found Ronald's jacket where the girl was buried. There was blood on the hem of the jacket. He left footprints on the grave and elsewhere, and they seem to match the basketball shoes we found in Ronald's room. We'll have to take them with us, of course. They're evidence. I don't have any doubt but what the soil in the treads will match the soil at the scene of the crime. And also —" he brought forth a sheet of paper "— this was in Ronald's room."

Mrs. Wilby took the paper. She knew what was there; she had dictated it herself and Ronald had written,

> Dear Mother:
> I've done something awful, and now I've got to leave and go somewhere far away. Please don't try to find me; I want to start a new life. If and when I can, I'll write you. I'm so very sorry to cause you unhappiness.
> All my love, your son,
> Ronald

Mrs. Wilby closed her eyes, half-convinced that Ronald had indeed written the note and had gone far away where she would never see him again. Oh, to be allowed to return twenty-four hours in time!

The two policemen remained politely silent until Mrs. Wilby opened her eyes. Lynch asked, "Has Ronald ever spoken of a place he particularly wanted to visit?"

"No," spoke Mrs. Wilby in a plangent, fateful voice. "Ronald is gone. If he did what you say he did…" She hesitated. The deed was unreal. The more they talked the more abstract it became. "I suppose the news will be in the papers, and all Ronald's friends will know?"

"I don't see how it can be avoided. You have my sympathy, Mrs. Wilby. Parents always suffer most — both sets of parents."

Mrs. Wilby had not yet considered the plight of the Mathews family. "I don't believe I know them." For some reason she could not bring herself to pronounce the name.

"Donald Mathews operates the Happy Valley Saloon on South Main Street. It's a very respectable place, incidentally. His son Duane used to be your paper boy."

Mrs. Wilby nodded without interest.

Lynch asked, "How much money would Ronald have with him?"

"I don't really know. Perhaps twenty or thirty dollars."

The policemen rose to their feet. "If Ronald communicates with you, we'll expect you to let us know at once."

Mrs. Wilby remained silent. She prided herself on her truthfulness and now found deceit very difficult indeed.

The police officers departed. A few minutes later Mrs. Wilby saw them next door, on Mrs. Schumacher's front porch, and presently they were admitted into the house. They'd get an earful there for sure! Mrs. Wilby thought of her job and the people with whom she worked. She thrust out her jaw. No help for it. If there were whispers and stares, she'd simply have to bear up and take no notice. As soon as possible, she and Ronald would quietly slip off to some far place and never think of Oakmead again. Until that day — well, at the very least she could dismiss her bleak fear of loneliness.

Mrs. Wilby felt upset to her stomach, almost queasy with tension and fatigue. She went around the house, wandering from room to room, looking out the windows. The police had departed. Almost certainly they'd maintain a watch on the house, and they'd probably keep her under surveillance as well. She'd have to be crafty and cunning, especially while shopping, since she'd still have to buy for two. And Mrs. Schumacher was always a threat. No doubt the police had asked her to keep her eyes peeled — as if Mrs. Schumacher needed any encouragement!

Mrs. Wilby at last went into the pantry and knelt down by the secret door. She rapped four times, and slid the door a few inches ajar. "Ronald?"

"Yes, Mother?"

"The police have been here."

"I heard them." Ronald's voice was peevish. "They don't sound too nice."

"They're only policemen doing their job. To them you're just like anyone else. We'll have to be very careful indeed."

"I realize that, Mother. I'm really sorry I'm making all this trouble. I just couldn't help it. It happened so quickly…"

"I know all about that. Push out your breakfast tray."

"I'd like my lunch. I'm really hungry. Is there any of that cake left?"

"I don't know what you'll do when I'm at work. But remember — under no circumstances come out! Mrs. Schumacher will be watching with her nose to the window, and the police will also be watching. If they see you, all our plans will go for nothing."

"I'll be careful. Can I flush the toilet now?"

"Just a minute. I'll go upstairs. When you hear the upstairs toilet, you flush yours. How is the air in there?"

"It's stuffy."

"Doesn't the fan over the toilet work?"

"It doesn't do much good. There's no place for air to come in."

"We'll have to figure something out. For now you'll just have to be uncomfortable. I'll go up and flush the toilet. Then I'll fix your lunch."

Chapter V

A WEEK PASSED, and two weeks. Mrs. Wilby went about her ordinary routines as placidly as she was able. At Central Valley Hardware she was admired for her dignity and fortitude: credit which she did not altogether deserve, for she had taken herself so deeply into her new existence that she was hardly aware of other people or their judgments. Two persons only were real: Ronald and herself. She worked toward a single goal: enough money to move away from California, perhaps to Canada, though how this could be achieved she was not quite sure.

At home Mrs. Wilby spent considerable time contriving economies. Ronald's requirements were now minimal except for food and whatever he needed to keep himself entertained. He wanted a small television with a set of earphones, which Mrs. Wilby refused to provide, citing the expense of such an instrument. Privately she felt that the television would provide far too much erotic stimulation for a person in his circumstances, and for which Ronald demonstrably had no need.

Mrs. Wilby had never squandered money on food, and now she spent less. Ronald made few complaints so long as he was served an ample dessert. Mrs. Wilby began to fear that Ronald might become seriously overweight, what with his inactivity and the rather starchy diet. She expressed her misgivings and recommended that Ronald not only eat less but undertake a regular regimen of exercise. Ronald rejected the suggestion out of hand. "It's too hard to exercise in here! There's not all that much room!"

"Nonsense, Ronald. You can do that running-in-place exercise, and all kinds of calisthenics. Certainly you don't want to become fat."

"Exercise just makes me hungry," Ronald grumbled. "I'd eat more."

"In that case, I'll have to cut down on your portions, and we'll forget about desserts. When we go east, we want you to be trim and healthy."

Ronald muttered something inaudible, but nonetheless began to exercise. Through some inexplicable quirk he became interested in the process, and Mrs. Wilby began to hear the regular thump of his feet as he ran in place. Indeed, she felt obliged to caution him. "When I'm not home, never run or jog, because the sound is quite noticeable, and there's also a vibration. The mailman might notice, or the man who reads the meter. Just do your push-ups and isometric exercises — anything that's absolutely quiet."

"When we have a new home, I'd like a room I could make into a gymnasium," said Ronald. "I might even take up weight lifting."

Mrs. Wilby had chanced upon a weight-lifting contest while turning the television dials, and had watched in fascinated disgust. "I don't know about that. Those people always look so grotesque. You just develop a good healthy body and never mind the weight lifting."

To Mrs. Wilby's relief, Ronald never expressed a desire to leave his lair, not even late at night when it might have been safe. Mrs. Wilby was afraid that if he left the lair even once, a precedent would be set, and Ronald would want to come forth at ever more frequent intervals, until by some freak of chance he would be noticed and his presence reported to the police. Better, far better, to play the game safely. They had worked so hard and sacrificed so much! Any relaxation would be sheer folly.

The issue never arose. Ronald felt comfortable and secure. The room was now adequately ventilated; he had broken a hole through the lath and plaster of the wall beside the toilet, which allowed a draught of air to enter from the attic, by way of the space between the studs. His meals were to his liking, if a trifle scant at times, but on the other hand he was no longer required to dry dishes. In fact, he had no responsibilities whatever, except to be utterly silent and to keep his weight down.

All, of course, was not a bed of roses. His mother's attitude did not altogether suit him. At times her tone of voice was just a bit peremptory and she tended to reiterate the most elementary instructions, as if she still considered him a child. That was just about the situation, thought Ronald wisely. His mother was competent in all things, but she had never reconciled herself to his growing up. The situation nonetheless had its compensations. Nothing too irksome was expected of him and if he coaxed long enough, he could usually get about what he wanted in the way of small treats. Matters could be a great deal worse, and if his mother wanted to baby him a bit, why spoil her pleasure? Ronald nodded sagely. This was generous and unselfish conduct on his part; he hoped his mother appreciated it. She enjoyed taking care of him, and until this unfortunate affair blew over she'd have ample opportunity to do so. Meanwhile, his little den was cozy and secure.

Ronald became obsessed with exercise. His mother drove into Stockton and bought some cheap exercising aids and a body-building manual, with which Ronald was very pleased. At his request she also supplied him a set of watercolors, a pad of good paper, ballpoint and felt-tip pens with various inks, as well as notebooks, a compass, a ruler and a dozen pencils. Ronald explained that he had long wanted to write and illustrate a history of the magic land Atranta and now seemed as good a time as any.

Mrs. Wilby gave only lukewarm encouragement to the project. She would have preferred that Ronald study biology and mathematics and anatomy, to prepare himself for the medical career to be undertaken after they had re-established themselves. Ronald agreed that the notion was sound, but when his mother brought him books on these subjects he showed little interest in them.

One Saturday about six weeks after his first visit Sergeant Lynch again dropped in on Mrs. Wilby. Hearing a car stop in front of the house, she looked out the window, then ran into the hall to rap sharply twice on the wall.

Lynch rang the bell; Mrs. Wilby opened the door and looked impassively forth.

"May I come in?" Lynch asked. "It's more comfortable than standing on the porch."

Mrs. Wilby silently took him into the living room. Lynch seated himself on the sofa.

Mrs. Wilby asked, "Have you been able to find Ronald?"

Lynch gave his head a slow sad shake. "Not a trace. Not even a whisper. It's as if he vanished into thin air, to coin a phrase. Have you heard from him, by any chance?"

Mrs. Wilby snorted almost derisively. "Wherever he is, I hope he lives a straight clean life, to make up for what happened here."

"I hope so, too, Mrs. Wilby. That would be practical rehabilitation, if it happened like that. Too often it doesn't, but we won't go into that."

Lynch leaned back and crossed his legs, apparently comfortable and in no hurry to leave. Mrs. Wilby sat tense and anxious, one ear straining for any sound that Ronald carelessly might make. What if he flushed the toilet now, for instance!

But silence prevailed. Lynch rose to his feet. "This is a real big house for just you to be rattling around in. Don't you get a little lonely?"

Mrs. Wilby managed a smile. "Believe it or not, after I work all day, I enjoy the quiet. I can do exactly what I want and when I want, which is worth a little loneliness."

"You might be right there. Well, I guess we haven't anything to tell each other, and I might as well be going. Don't forget to call me if you hear from Ronald."

Mrs. Wilby could not restrain a question. "Have you seen his father?"

Lynch nodded. "He was very disturbed, as you might imagine. But he knows nothing of Ronald's whereabouts, or so he claims." Lynch grinned. "Naturally we take the assertions of a parent with a grain of salt."

"I'm sure you know your business," said Mrs. Wilby, somewhat tartly.

"I'm not Sergeant Lynch for nothing. And if I don't produce results, I might be just plain Deputy Lynch again and in very short order. That's the way it goes. Goodby, Mrs. Wilby."

"Goodby." Mrs. Wilby watched through the window as Lynch got into his car and drove away. She walked around the house as before, looking out all the windows. The coast seemed to be clear. How she hated this conniving and working against the law! She who had never so much as incurred a traffic citation in her entire life! What a sorry mess! But if it meant having Ronald here with her instead of in some horrid jail full of sexual degenerates, any sacrifice was worthwhile. What was the phrase Sergeant Lynch had used? 'Practical rehabilitation'. Exactly what she was achieving. Ronald essentially was a dreamy, impractical boy who needed his mother to look after him, and probably would always do so. The idea gave Mrs. Wilby a flush of pleasure. It was nice to feel necessary in a world so cold and impersonal.

She went into the pantry and tapped four times on the door, which Ronald raised up. They had long since fitted hinges and a latch on the panel, and the secret door now functioned in a most convenient manner. "The police were just here," said Mrs. Wilby. "I think it was just a routine call, but once again it shows how careful we must be!"

"We're just too clever for them," declared Ronald. "You're really a wonderful actress!"

"I'm nothing of the sort," snapped Mrs. Wilby. This gloating jocularity was definitely not the tone she wanted Ronald to take. She wondered if he really appreciated the seriousness of the situation. He certainly evinced none of the restlessness and melancholy which would have made both their lives harder but which would have reassured her. To the contrary, he seemed quite happy eating, reading, sleeping, exercising and working on his imaginary history. She made up her mind to crack down on Ronald. She would insist that he study science and mathematics. But not just now; she was in no mood for argument. In the tension of Sergeant Lynch's visit she had forgotten to take her digestive tablet, and now she did so. Her stomach still felt twisted and queasy. The last thing she wanted was an ulcer!

She fixed dinner for herself and Ronald, and afterwards calculated how long it would be before they could consider leaving. Originally she had reckoned in terms of a few months, six months at the most, but money accumulated so slowly! They'd want at least two thousand dollars; she'd hate to leave with less. A year? By that time the furore and scandal would be forgotten. They could make an unobtrusive move and no one would be the wiser.

So — a target date of a year. A very long time, but the longer they remained in Oakmead, the better their chance for a successful new start in life. It was hard on Ronald of course. Poor dear Ronald! He had been such a cunning little chap. Who would have foreseen the terrible tragedy, which might have blighted his life had she not been able to help him! A year would go by very swiftly; she'd have the necessary two thousand dollars, or perhaps even three thousand — if she could cut down even more on expenses. For instance — life insurance premiums. They'd be taking new identities. What good was the old insurance? She'd cash it in at once. Ronald's health insurance was now a useless expenditure. She'd cancel that, and her own as well, and save another precious thirty-five dollars a month. Ronald's requirements for clothes, recreation and miscellaneous needs were now almost nil. Her own clothes were cheap and serviceable, and if she needed anything new, perhaps she'd try to sew for herself. After this month she'd stop the newspaper and renew no magazine subscriptions, and somewhere she'd heard that soybean meal made a cheap and nutritious meat extender. Well worth a trial, since meat was so high. The telephone? Mrs. Wilby deliberated, and decided against terminating service; sometimes she needed to call the office. But she could easily change to a party-line, limited-use basis. It all added up! Perhaps someday, when Ronald was rich and successful, they'd take a trip to Europe; she'd always wanted to visit Venice and Paris and the stately homes of England; and then perhaps they would be able to laugh at the dark times through which they were now passing. Or would either care to bring the subject up? Hmmf. Probably not.

Chapter VI

The magic land of Atranta comprised six domains: Kastifax, Hangkill, Fognor, Dismark, Plume and Chult, each dominated by a wizard duke. Each duke lived in a grand castle, with turrets, towers and barbicans above and evil dungeons below. At the center of Atranta was wonderful Zulamber, the City of Blue-green Pearls, ruled by Fansetta, a beautiful pearl and gold princess. The wizard dukes conducted interminable wars, one against the other, using magic weapons, troops of weirds, ghouls and imps, and when not so occupied plotted against Princess Fansetta. An ancient legend prophesied that the man to win Fansetta's love would rule all Atranta; for this reason Fansetta's chastity, life and very soul were in constant danger.

Into Atranta from the far land Vordling has come Norbert, a fugitive from the tyrant of Vordling and himself a prince. By dint of craft and daring Norbert has defeated Urken, Wizard Duke of Kastifax and taken possession of his magic castle and all his wizardly spells.

Fansetta, Princess of Zulamber, the City of Blue-green Pearls, has seen Norbert in her magic lens and fallen in love with him, even though she thinks he is Urken...

RONALD HAD NOT YET developed the story beyond this stage; too many exciting possibilities existed. Furthermore, a great deal of preliminary work must be done: first, the detailed history of Atranta, with the genealogy of all the wizard duchies; the waxing and waning of their powers across the years; the ancient founding of the city Zulamber and the posting of the Guardians with their Seven Spells; the histories of all the various princesses who had come to power in Zulamber. All were fey, and their lives were not as delightful as one might expect, since Zulamber, the single great city of Atranta, was a hive of intrigue and derring-do. Secondly, the Grand Map of Atranta, which covered the wall across from Ronald's cot, was not yet complete, although Ronald had already lavished many hours of loving care upon the project. The scale was five miles to the inch; Ronald used pens of the finest nib and the most subtle gradations of color to depict every feature of the quaint and marvelous landscape: the rise and elevation of every hill, crag, knoll, ridge and cliff; the course of each river and rill; the extent of the Dismal Desert, the Windy Waste and the Fearful Fells. He plotted each road, lane and foot-path; he laid out each town and hamlet and indicated each landmark, monument, battleground, castle, fort, cave, sarsen, and megalith. As he worked, he compiled an index, listing places and coordinates. A work of enormous scope, but which afforded Ronald much satisfaction. After all, he was in no great hurry, and never before had so much spare time been available. Spare time? Ha! What with his exercises, the Grand Map, the History, his sketches of the castles of the Wizard Dukes, he barely had time to listen to the radio, much less study the dust-dry textbooks his mother brought him. Sometimes he wasn't even sure that he wanted to be a doctor. A pity his mother didn't make more money. Maybe his Aunt Margaret would die and leave them all her wealth. Unfortunately his cousins Earl and Agnes would get it all. Hmm, things might be different, Ronald reflected, if Earl and Agnes died before Aunt Margaret. But they lived far away in Pennsylvania. Earl and Agnes no doubt by now had heard of his 'wicked deed' and his 'disappearance'. If only they knew! Agnes was a rather pretty girl. Cousin or not, he wouldn't mind having her in to share his lair. She'd have to be quiet, of course, but they could have a fine time together. Even better would be that treacherous little bitch Laurel Hansen. How he hated her; how he'd love to get his hands on her! Fansetta, the Pearl Princess, rather resembled Laurel, and no doubt she'd get her comeuppance somewhere in the story — probably at the hands of Gangrod, one of the most evil and sadistic of the Wizard Dukes. Norbert, of course, would rescue her, but Norbert might then be in love with Shallis, a dark-haired beggar girl, exquisitely pretty in spite of rags and dirt and certain sordid habits. Shallis looked a little bit like Laurel too, come to think of it. He seemed to have Laurel on the mind...Laurel, Laurel, that wicked little schemer! It was essentially her fault that he was here in his lair! No one would believe this if he explained it. Jeering feckless Laurel wouldn't believe it either, that was sure, and wouldn't care anyway. Some day she'd suffer, as much or more than he had suffered! Though for a fact his lair was quite snug and comfortable, and he had no responsibilities to distract him from the things he wanted to do. He'd like bigger helpings at meal-times, and more luscious desserts — he was getting just a bit tired of jello — but this was a minor complaint. His mother was right; he didn't want to become fat. Not too fat anyway. Despite everything he had gained a little weight. If he wanted to crawl out into the kitchen while his mother was gone, he could always find something to eat. But he didn't care to leave his lair; if once he left, it would somehow change things. The coziness would be gone. Also, his mother had strictly warned him against coming out; someone might see him. His mother knew best; he'd keep to his lair where he had his work, his exercise, his meals. Life was effortless; he was content.

Chapter VII

One Saturday afternoon in November, Mrs. Wilby went to do her week's shopping at the supermarket. At the pharmaceutical shelf she halted to look for a new digestive medicine she had seen advertised on television, for her old preparation was not giving the relief she expected. A thin nervous-looking woman of about her own age, with dark hair and expressive dark eyes, came down the aisle. At her side was a rather solemn lad perhaps a year older than Ronald, evidently her son. Seeing Mrs. Wilby he muttered something to his mother.

Finding the price of the medicine excessive, Mrs. Wilby turned to move on, and pushed her shopping cart into that of the other woman. She said, "Excuse me," and would have continued, but the other woman spoke to her in a quick anxious voice. "Aren't you Mrs. Wilby?"

"Why yes, I am," Mrs. Wilby could not quite place the woman. Perhaps Ronald had known her son, a medium-sized lad with an erect posture and a keen, rather bony face. For a fact, he looked familiar.

"I'm Mrs. Mathews. This is my son Duane, but I expect you already know him. He delivered your paper."

"Of course," said Mrs. Wilby, rather lamely. "I remember him very well." She felt hot and embarrassed; the last person in the world she wanted to chat with was Mrs. Mathews, even had her husband not been the owner of a saloon.

"I've often thought about calling you," said Mrs. Mathews in a rush of words. "I know how you must feel about that awful business. You must be suffering far more than we are, and I wanted you to know that you have our deepest sympathy."

Mrs. Wilby finally found words. "That's very kind of you, Mrs.

Mathews, and you're right: we share the tragedy. I've decided that I simply can't brood, that I've got to go on living, and this is what I'm trying to do."

Mrs. Mathews' eyes glistened, and she took an impulsive step forward. Mrs. Wilby feared that she was either about to break into tears, or attempt an embrace, either of which would have embarrassed her dreadfully. But Mrs. Mathews controlled herself. She said simply, "The Lord has His reasons. He does nothing without cause, and it's presumptuous for us to question His wisdom."

"Yes, I suppose that's right."

"Still, for both our sakes, I can't help but wish that the Lord in His mercy had arranged things differently."

Mrs. Wilby bowed her head in agreement, wishing that Mrs. Mathews would get along with her shopping and allow her to do the same. Her cart was loaded with food: three pounds of hamburger, five pounds of rice, two chickens, two loaves of bread, a pound of margarine, two large cartons of chocolate milk, three heads of lettuce, which were on special, and it seemed that Duane Mathews was inspecting her purchases with something other than casual interest. "I'm so pleased to have spoken to you," said Mrs. Wilby and with a smile for Duane moved off down the aisle.

That evening she was unusually short with Ronald, who grumbled at his dessert. "Do we have to have jello every night? I thought you were going to get some ice cream."

For a fact, Mrs. Wilby had promised to do so, but after meeting Mrs. Mathews, she had come away without buying all she intended. "Please don't complain, Ronald. I do the best I can, and you don't help matters by being finicky." Implicit was the idea that any disappointment Ronald felt at the lack of ice cream derived from his own conduct.

Ronald said no more, but the evening was quite spoiled for him. After dinner, he lay sulkily listening to the radio. His mother needn't have been so sharp; after all, he had apologized for that wretched affair not once, but several times. She failed to appreciate him just like everyone else. As for Carol Mathews, in the final analysis, she was as much at fault as himself; if she hadn't been so defiant and revengeful things would have gone differently. Perhaps it wasn't logical to blame

Laurel Hansen either; still, logic or not, that's what he felt, and perhaps someday…He heaved a deep sigh. No, he didn't want to get in any more trouble. When they moved to Florida he'd simply have to forget her.

For Thanksgiving Mrs. Wilby roasted a small turkey, and prepared sweet potatoes candied in pineapple syrup with marshmallows on top the way Ronald liked best. It would have been wonderful to pull all the drapes and bring Ronald out so that they might enjoy a real Thanksgiving dinner together — but better not. If Ronald were allowed out on one occasion, he might want to come out at every pretext, and sooner or later someone would learn their secret. So Ronald had his Thanksgiving dinner served on a tray, but he was allowed as much as he wanted of everything. Mrs. Wilby herself ate very little. Her ulcer, as she now diagnosed her difficulty, was causing her discomfort, and perhaps she'd better go see a doctor, though how she hated to spend the money! Christmas was coming up, which meant expense, no matter how she tried to avoid it: Christmas cards and postage, a gift for the office party, presents for Ronald, a tree — well, perhaps not a tree this year. In fact, she'd definitely do without a tree. And Ronald's presents would be absolutely minimal. There was not only the expense to be considered, but also the fact that when they departed Oakmead, they'd perforce go with the bare necessities. In fact, a month or so before the departure date, she might discreetly try to sell her furniture and appliances…On second thought, better not. Much too dangerous, if the police were still watching her. She had observed no evidence of surveillance, but it was hard to believe that they'd give up quite so easily. If they learned that she'd sold her furniture they'd know that she was planning to leave. Probably (so they'd think) to join Ronald, and they would keep a careful watch upon all her actions.

She explained to Ronald that Christmas this year must be very quiet and Ronald made no protest. For a fact, there was nothing he wanted except a small television set, and perhaps a subscription to *Playboy* — futile hopes, both.

"Don't get me anything at all," he insisted. "It's more important that we save the money. But I'd like you to get something for yourself, something that you want, so that I'd feel that you were having a nice Christmas."

Mrs. Wilby was touched. "We'll never have a nice Christmas until we're far away from Oakmead, where no one knows us. If you really want to make this a nice Christmas for me, you'll start studying. All this leisure could be put to good use, if you'd try."

Ronald said humbly, "I know you're right. After the holidays I'll really buckle down. There's no use neglecting my education."

"Of course not! I don't know how we'll get you back in school; usually they want transcripts. Perhaps we'll try a private academy where they won't be so involved in red tape."

Christmas was not altogether drab. Mrs. Wilby bought a toy tree for Ronald's lair, and she roasted another small turkey, which was cheaper and went farther than steak or roast pork, which Ronald would have preferred. She couldn't bear to give Ronald no present whatever, and so bought him a bottle of *Wild Cossack* cologne, a book of crossword puzzles, and a very intricate jigsaw puzzle.

Ronald was profuse in his thanks. "I really didn't want anything, but these are all great! I hope you bought yourself something."

"Yes, dear, I did. I needed underwear very badly and I treated myself to some nice new things."

"Good! I'm glad! You should have gotten more!"

Mrs. Wilby's Christmas dinner was solitary and sad. How different from the old times, when she and Ronald had shared the joy of Christmas together! From sheer boredom she ate more than usual, and shortly after dinner felt an acute nausea, which persisted on and off throughout the evening.

The next day she decided that she could tolerate the pain in her abdomen no longer and went to the doctor.

Late in the afternoon Mrs. Wilby returned home. Through the thin plasterboard which covered the old doorway Ronald heard her footsteps as she mounted the outside steps. He heard the front door open and close, then there was silence. Evidently his mother was standing motionless in the front hall. Strange, thought Ronald, who had developed a peculiarly keen awareness of atmosphere and moods. An alarming idea came to him: was it really his mother who stood out there? He rose quickly to his feet, like a great stealthy cat, and put his ear to the plasterboard. After a moment or two the person in the hall walked into the dining room. Yes, it was his mother; the rhythm of her footsteps was unmistakable, though she sounded tired and dispirited.

Mrs. Wilby peered out all the windows as was her invariable habit, but then, rather than rapping four times on the wall, she took a seat at the dining-room table. Inside the lair Ronald listened with mounting uneasiness. But he dared not call out to ask what was wrong; he must wait until his mother rapped four times. He sat down on his cot. Something was not as it should be.

Presently his mother came into the pantry and tapped four times on the secret door; Ronald quickly pulled it open. "Is anything wrong?"

Mrs. Wilby replied in a steady and controlled voice. "Yes, to some extent. The doctor says I have something wrong with my gall bladder, and I've got to have an operation."

Ronald crouched silently while he considered implications. "You mean you'll have to go to the hospital?"

"Yes. For at least a week and probably longer."

Again Ronald reflected. "When will you go?"

"Next week, on Monday."

"Well, I hope it makes you feel better," said Ronald with hollow cheerfulness.

"Oh, I'll feel better. I'm not worried about that. It's the money. Such things are ruinously expensive, and we don't have health insurance anymore."

Ronald ruminated. "How much will it cost?"

"I don't know exactly. As much as seven or eight hundred dollars I should imagine."

"Hmm." Ronald could think of nothing to say. His mother spoke in a flat voice, "I'll get you a hot-plate and plenty of food. You'll just have to take care of yourself while I'm gone."

"Certainly. That's all right, Mother. There's nothing to worry about."

"Except money."

Ronald grimaced. He hated the word 'money'. "Well, the most important thing is your health, no matter what it costs."

"I realize that. We'll just have to do the best we can."

CHAPTER VIII

ON THE FOLLOWING DAY Mrs. Wilby drove into Stockton, where the Canned Goods Discount Retailers sold packaged food products by the case at very reasonable prices. Mrs. Wilby was so impressed by the economies to be gained that she bought a case each of pork and beans, tamales, packaged macaroni and cheese dinners, and half-cases of peaches, pears and peas. She noticed ten-pound parcels of dry milk, which from now on Ronald must drink; chocolate milk was much too expensive and must be considered a luxury.

The store almost dazzled her with its array of bargains, and she resolved to return after her visit to the hospital. By dint of careful planning, she calculated that she could cut their food budget by perhaps a third even from its already low level. Ronald would hardly dare grumble, but to mollify him she bought an assortment of very reasonable soft drink powders and a dozen packages of devil's-food cupcakes. At a nearby hardware store she bought a cheap hot-plate, on which Ronald could cook his own meals, and then she returned home.

Here another problem presented itself: how to transport her carful of provisions into the house without exciting Mrs. Schumacher's curiosity?

Mrs. Wilby waited until dusk, when through the lighted windows she could see Mrs. Schumacher preparing dinner; then she hurried back and forth, from porch to automobile and in a very few minutes she had conveyed all her purchases inside.

As she expected, Ronald turned up his nose at the dry milk. Mrs. Wilby spoke sharply, "It's this or nothing! All the nutrition and minerals are there. It's the same except for water, which is a very expensive ingredient when you buy it in milk — or in any other food, for that matter."

Mrs. Wilby pushed the hot-plate and an ample supply of food through the secret door, and now her mind was easier. "Your meals won't be exciting, but at least you'll be able to feed yourself until I get back."

Ronald was suddenly apprehensive. "I hate to see you go for so long."

"It's unavoidable," said Mrs. Wilby crisply. "Please don't be difficult, Ronald. It's a case of either going to the hospital or becoming very ill indeed. I don't like it any more than you do."

On Monday morning Mrs. Wilby left for the hospital, after giving Ronald final instructions. "Now, dear, don't worry and don't fret. You have your books and your studies and your radio to keep you occupied. The time will go by very swiftly if you don't mope. Naturally, you won't leave the lair under any circumstances. For instance, I don't want you coming out to watch television or anything like that. Mrs. Schumacher is the busiest woman alive and she just might notice the light, or see you moving around. I've given you eight oranges, eight apples and eight nice raw carrots: eat one of each every day, and don't forget to take your vitamin pill. Don't neglect your exercises, and do get started on your studies. It's really very important if you ever want to make anything of yourself. Is everything clear now?"

Ronald said in a muffled voice, "Yes, Mother."

"All right then. I'll be going. And do behave yourself. Close down your secret door as soon as I'm gone."

Ronald made no reply. He heard his mother's steps: through the kitchen, the dining room, the hall. The front door opened, closed. She was gone. He was alone.

Ronald closed the secret door. He lay on his cot listening. The house was breathlessly quiet: a lonesome silence, very different from that during the days when his mother worked.

Ronald picked up one of the books his mother wanted him to study: *An Introduction to Algebra*. It looked difficult and very dull. Another book was *The Living World*, in which he found some interesting illustrations. The third book was *Men Against Death*, which described the lives of a dozen eminent doctors, medical experimenters and biologists.

Ronald pursed his lips and put the volume aside. He didn't want to be a doctor. What did he want to be? He hadn't made up his mind yet.

The morning passed very slowly. For lunch, Ronald fixed himself peanut butter and jelly sandwiches, and for dessert ate two packages of cupcakes. He mixed a glass of dry milk and drank it without enthusiasm. So much for lunch.

He busied himself with Atranta. Each of the six wizard-castles was to be sketched and rendered in watercolor; the interior plans were also to be detailed, from dungeons and torture chambers to the garrets. Ronald also planned to draw views of the main hall in each castle, and a full-length portrait of each Wizard Duke. By dint of painstaking trial and error he had already produced pencil sketches of the wizard-castles which he thought very effective. With human figures and faces he was less successful. He simply must practice until he got the knack; every day he'd work to train his hand, copying figures in the newspaper fashion advertisements.

The afternoon dragged past. Ronald became restless. His usual occupations failed to interest him. He exercised without zest, examined the Great Map of Atranta, and for a few minutes busied himself tracing a path across Cloud-Shadow Moor.

Even though Ronald could not glimpse the outdoors from within his lair, he felt the special qualities of morning, afternoon, evening and night; some indefinable aspect of his lair altered as the day progressed; and when dusk had darkened around the house, Ronald was quite aware of the fact. Gingerly he raised the secret door and looked out into the pantry. The sense of vacancy was exceedingly strong. His presence did not make itself felt; he was like a ghost. Ronald shivered. He closed the secret door, and cooked dinner over the hot-plate: tamales and beans, with bread and butter, a glass of the odious reconstructed milk, two more cupcakes and a banana.

Now it was night. Ronald wondered about his mother and whether the operation were over with. He knew she'd be thinking about him. He looked at the secret door again. His mother was really over-cautious. Certainly no harm could result from his leaving the lair, if he were careful. It was dark; no one could possibly see him. It would be fun to stretch his legs for a bit. Why not? His mother need never know.

He raised the secret door and started to crawl forth, when he noticed the glow of light reaching out ahead of him and into the pantry. Hastily he drew back and slammed the secret door. How careless could a person be? Probably no harm had been done; Mrs. Schumacher would have to be watching very intently to have noticed anything.

He extinguished his light, again raised the secret door, and crept out into the pantry. Slowly he hunched up on his hands and knees, and slowly rose to his feet. Hardly daring to breathe, he looked out into the kitchen. A streetlight about fifty yards down the street cast a pale illumination through the windows, somewhat less bright than moonlight, but exactly right for Ronald's mood. He stepped forth into the kitchen, thrilling with excitement. The Schumacher house was dark; perhaps they had gone out for the evening.

Ronald stole into the dining room: a place once so familiar and now like a strange and forbidden land. Ronald stood quivering with a peculiar excitement. He felt strange and strong and mysterious, like a supernatural being endowed with awful powers. No one knew of his existence; he could do as he wished; no one could stop him. He was beyond the control of any human agency!

On soft feet he slid into the living room. Through the front windows came slantwise shafts of pallid light. The submarine eye of the television stared at him from across the room. The sofa, the armchairs and escritoire stood in their appointed places: elemental entities, fixed and immutable.

I am alone, thought Ronald. I am unseen. I am a spirit of darkness, more than human! I have known more-than-human passion; I have done the forbidden deed! Human qualms no longer deter me, I know no human fears! And now an awesome enlightenment floated up from the depths of his mind: he was not sorry for what he had done to Carol Mathews. How could he be sorry for such wonderful fun! A pity only that he had blundered! Ronald drew and exhaled a deep breath. Moving closer to the windows, he peered out into the night. Somewhere out there was Laurel Hansen; probably in her house, but who knows? She might be coming home from some errand or a visit to a friend's house. Now there would be fun indeed! Oh Laurel, what anguish you have caused me! And Laurel, Laurel — what I would do to you if I could find you and take you somewhere alone!

But he dared not sally forth into the night. The streetlamp would shine upon his unmasked face; he might be seen and recognized, and then all the town would get up a hue and cry. He would be harried and chased and finally driven to bay…No, no, best not leave the house!

Fifteen minutes he stood in the living room, then he returned through the hall and into the dining room. He sat down at the table and breathed the odor of waxed wood and varnish and the sublimated essence of ten thousand dinners.

Ronald sat enjoying the silence. At last he arose, went back through the kitchen, with its own distinctive smell, into the pantry, down to the floor and back through the secret door into his lair. He closed the secret door; now he could turn on his light and return to human life! Here was the brain of the house, the pulsing node of intelligence and passion, here in this secret inner chamber, where he lived unseen and unknown!

He stretched out on his cot and lay staring up at the ceiling. It occurred to him that the secret room was complete except for one deficiency, which he would remedy as soon as possible — and keep secret even from his mother.

Ronald awoke early to a sense of excitement, for events whose imminence he could feel but not define.

He breakfasted on cereal and bananas, and meanwhile inspected the floor of his lair, which was covered with a checkerboard of yellow and white vinyl tile. After breakfast he deliberated a few minutes, then opened his secret door and looked warily forth. Sunlight streamed into the kitchen; a half-dozen flies buzzed against the window panes. Ronald crawled out into the pantry, across the kitchen, and out upon the back porch.

Over the years Mrs. Wilby had accumulated an assortment of household tools. Ronald selected a chisel, a hammer, a brace and bit, a keyhole saw and an ordinary crosscut saw. Moving on hands and knees, he conveyed these back across the kitchen, through the pantry, into his lair.

With the chisel he pried up a number of the floor tiles and scraped away the mastic to reveal the old tongue-and-groove floorboards. With the brace and bit he drilled several holes until he located a joist, then set to work with first the keyhole saw, then the regular saw. Both were rusty and dull; sawing was slow work, especially since he felt impelled to muffle the sound with a towel.

Ronald worked all morning, without haste. He dared not use hammer and nails; wherever necessary he used screws. When he was finished, he had constructed a trapdoor which permitted him access to the crawl-space below the house, and thence to the outside world through the lattice-work door beside the steps to the back porch.

Ronald carefully gathered all the shavings and splintered wood from the ground below the trapdoor. The trapdoor, so he determined, was difficult to detect unless a person were specifically looking for such a thing.

Ronald took the tools back to the porch, returned to his lair, and prepared a good lunch for himself. The trapdoor allowed him an extra dimension of flexibility, should the need arise. Today Ronald did not quite like to define what such a need might be, but it was always best to be ready for anything.

At about one o'clock Ronald crawled through the dining room into the hall, where he rose to his feet. Through the dining room window he watched Mrs. Schumacher come out of her house and change the sprinkler on her lawn. The Schumachers were very proud of their beautiful green lawn and constantly watered, mowed and clipped — always where they could look directly into the Wilby dining room. His mother had not exaggerated the need for vigilance.

He sidled into the living room and lying flat on the rug watched a football game on television, refreshing himself with orange-flavored drink and peanut butter sandwiches. The sound he kept down to the merest whisper.

When dusk came, he switched off the television for fear that the flicker might be noticed from the street. He returned on hands and knees to his lair and cooked a package of macaroni and cheese for his dinner. He mixed powdered chocolate into his reconstructed milk, vastly improving the flavor.

He lay on his cot, reflecting almost complacently upon the circumstances of his life. Things weren't all that bad. No school, no chores, plenty of time for relaxation. He thought about Carol Mathews and hissed through his teeth. He turned out his light, opened the secret door, and once more slid forth from the lair, to move like a ghost through the house. The new trapdoor augmented his might. He could be in and out, if he so chose, and no one would know of his weird comings and goings… He stood by the front window, looking out into the street. He wondered if there were a crawl-space under the Hansen house. He grimaced. The street-light was his enemy! Still, if he dressed in dark clothes and walked quickly north, away from the light, no one would ever notice. And even if he were seen, who would recognize him? For his hair had grown long, and he looked like a hippie.

But he simply lacked the courage to go forth from the house. Suppose that he found Laurel, or another girl, and, well, something happened and his mother found out about it, she'd be very annoyed. Ronald blew out his cheeks. She wouldn't tell the police, or anything like that, but she'd certainly punish him in some very unpleasant fashion — cut out his desserts for months on end.

Too much risk was involved. Perhaps he had never seriously planned to go forth in the first place. Although if a girl passed in front of the house — well, it might be worth the risk to dart out and make a capture. Ronald peered up and down the street.

Across the room the telephone jangled. Ronald jerked in terror. He took a quick step toward the phone, to take the receiver from the hook and stop the terrible noise. He drew back just in time. Let it ring! It was probably a wrong number, or someone who didn't know his mother was sick. Let it ring. This noise was no threat.

But how he hated that jangle! Somewhere someone waited with a receiver to his or her ear. Who could be calling? Ronald would never know. Somewhere someone decided that no one was home and hung up the receiver, and the phone at last became quiet. The house seemed more lonesome than ever, and somewhat dreary. Ronald went back to his lair, closed the secret door, turned on the light, and lay listening to his radio.

Chapter IX

Mrs. Wilby finally came home from the hospital. Ronald heard the key in the lock and the creak of the door opening. He quickly closed his secret door and stood with his ear to the wall, to make sure that the entrant was his mother and not some stranger.

He recognized his mother's footsteps. They were slower and less crisp than before. Mrs. Wilby was still weak, and still dejected by the size of the bill.

She came directly into the pantry and rapped four times on the secret door. "Ronald, I'm home. Ronald?"

Ronald lifted the secret door. "I'm here. How are you?"

"Oh, well enough. I feel a bit weak, and I'm not supposed to work until next Monday at the earliest. How have you managed?"

"Very well. It's been lonely, but I guess it couldn't be helped."

"Definitely not." Mrs. Wilby's voice was dry. "I'm lucky I went in when I did. I had what is called 'cholelithiasis'—gall-stones, and the surgeon removed my gall bladder. The bill was appalling. The thought of it makes me sick all over again."

"Don't worry about it," Ronald advised. "The main thing is your health."

"I realize that. Still, the expense has set us back, and I want so desperately to leave this town, and start life over again. Have you been studying?"

Ronald pursed his lips. "Yes, quite a bit."

"Hmmf." Mrs. Wilby's tone was skeptical, but she did not pursue the subject. "I can't think of any way to get more money. We've got nothing to sell ... We'll just have to grit our teeth and do everything we can to save."

"I suppose that means more dry milk?" Traces of petulance, self-pity, and even sarcasm could be heard in Ronald's voice.

"Yes," said Mrs. Wilby. "It means more dry milk, and anything else which might save us a few cents. You've got to do your part too, Ronald."

"You don't drink milk, so it doesn't mean anything to you," Ronald grumbled. "That stuff tastes like chalk."

"I'll give up coffee and tea, which aren't really necessary. The hardship will bear on us both. You've just got to face up to facts, Ronald. We've got to put aside every possible cent, and get out of here as soon as we can because this is the time you should be in school preparing for a career. You say that you've been studying?"

"Yes, of course."

"Have you done the exercises in the algebra book?"

"It's not all that necessary. I study the examples and make sure I understand them. There's no real reason to wade through all the routine."

"You start at the beginning of the book and do every single problem! Then you can pass the papers out to me, and I'll check them. You have all the time in the world. It's shameful that you don't use it to advantage!"

"I do the best I can," growled Ronald. "I've got my exercises and my art work and, well, other things that take up time."

Mrs. Wilby gave a grim laugh. "I suggest that you organize your time around your studies, rather than making them an afterthought. You've got to jack yourself up, Ronald. I realize that it's very tiresome for you, but you've got to keep up your morale! That means acting in such a way that you can take pride in yourself and I can be proud of you. Have you bathed since I've been gone?"

Ronald was supposed to take a sponge bath in the basin every day or so.

"I wash whenever I feel dirty," said Ronald. "It's not too comfortable, trying to wash in that little basin. I get all wet and clammy."

"Ronald, it's absolutely important that you don't let yourself go. Even in the tropics an English gentleman dresses for dinner. It's his pride in himself and his good breeding. Now I know that you're not an English gentleman, but you can certainly take the lesson to heart. I hate to say this, Ronald, but your lair doesn't smell all that well. You've got to tidy up. Put your head down where I can see you."

"What do you want to see my head for?"

"Don't argue, Ronald! Do as I say!"

Ronald grudgingly put his head into the aperture. Mrs. Wilby sniffed. "Just stay there till I get scissors."

"What are you going to do?"

"I'm going to cut your hair. Then I'm going to buy you a razor, and you can shave those straggling wisps around your mouth."

"Wait a minute! Long hair is in style now, and so are beards and mustaches!"

"You hardly need to concern yourself with 'style'."

Ronald said no more, and Mrs. Wilby chopped off a good pint of Ronald's lank curls. "Now," said Mrs. Wilby, "pass out all your bed things and all your dirty clothes and I'll give them a good wash. Meanwhile you mop the floor. I'll get you a bucket of soap and water and Clorox. Then I want you to give yourself a good scrubbing."

Sullenly Ronald cleaned the floor of his lair, and was somewhat surprised to see the water became opaque with dirt. Where did it all come from? A mystery.

He washed himself and dressed in clean pajamas. His mother brought him clean linen and he made up his cot. He more or less agreed that the room smelled fresher, and for a fact the clean pajamas felt crisp and smooth rather than limp and sticky, but what he objected to was his mother's attitude. She acted as if the whole thing were his fault. Well — perhaps it was, but that business was far in the past, and it wasn't fair to keep taking him to task about everything. Life was starting to seem bleak. Books, studying, poor food, this unreasonable emphasis upon everything being spic and span. And why all the haste to move to Canada or Maryland or Florida? Was it worth the trouble if they couldn't eat properly, or buy chocolate milk once in a while? He wasn't definitely set on becoming a doctor, and if not, all the effort of studying algebra and doing those tedious problems was just time down the drain. It didn't seem sensible to waste energy in preparation for a career which he might never pursue! But impossible to talk logic to his mother. Ronald sighed, and wondered whether she'd expect him to do the problems today. She was just home from the hospital! They should celebrate, forget about expense for a day or two!

"Mother," called Ronald softly.

Mrs. Wilby came into the pantry. "Ronald, you must never, *never* do that again! We don't have many visitors, but every once in a while someone is here. Never, never, never call out like that, even if you are sure we are alone — because you might be mistaken. Now what did you want?"

"I was thinking that it would be nice to celebrate your coming out of the hospital. Why don't we have a little party, or something of the sort? You can make a nice cake, and maybe cook barbecued spareribs and baked potatoes with butter…"

"Ronald," said Mrs. Wilby, "do you know what butter costs a pound? And what we'd have to pay for spareribs — which are all bone to begin with? Prices are just outrageous."

"Just for today we could forget about prices. I'm really awfully glad to have you home."

"It wouldn't be any celebration for me. I can't eat rich foods, or fats, or oils. The doctor put me on a strict diet. I'm really not all that well yet."

"Oh."

"I'm going to rest a bit now, and while it's quiet, you can get busy with your algebra. You've wasted quite enough time on your drawings. It's time to come back to earth. You can't make a career of dreams, you know. You've got to work with people, and serve people. It's hard work, and you might as well get at it right now."

A week later Mrs. Wilby made another visit to the Canned Goods Discount Retailers in Stockton and bought another carload of cheap food. Ronald loved peanut butter, a cheap and nutritious meat substitute; she bought three gallons of the substance, and also a gallon of catsup, a sack of beans, another case of macaroni and cheese dinners, twenty-five pounds of rice, a case of canned tuna, a case of canned frankfurters, and half-cases of various other items which she considered sound value, including two twenty-pound cartons of dry milk.

She drove home with a degree of wan satisfaction. She had spent a good deal of money, but she had secured a fine supply of wholesome food, enough to last several months, supplemented of course with hamburger and fresh vegetables… She recalled reading that a number of wild plants provided excellent spinach-like greens: the dandelion, wild mustard and alfalfa. She'd certainly have to check for the availability of these greens when growing weather began.

Once again she waited till dark to unload her supplies, and when everything had been carried into the house she felt exhausted. The illness had taken a great deal of her strength, and she wasn't growing any younger. But she couldn't relax, couldn't let down, couldn't give in an inch until they were comfortably resettled in Florida. So tomorrow: back to work. And Ronald must concentrate upon studies. She had tolerated his dillydallying long enough.

Chapter X

Ronald detested history; he despised biology; he loathed mathematics. Nevertheless every day except Sunday he was expected to produce evidence that he had completed what his mother considered a fair amount of work. She was an exacting taskmaster. Ronald must write resumés of the material he studied, in good writing, and in his own words. She allowed no vagueness or double-talk. If Ronald made a mistake in his mathematics, she gave him ten more problems of the same sort, and she insisted upon neatness. Ronald cursed and sulked and thought that school was never as hard as this.

His mother seemed to have changed. She was certainly less sympathetic with his wants and preferences, and sometimes even a bit sharp. Not that she loved him the less, of this he was sure, but she seemed preoccupied and worried, and almost overnight she looked ten years older. Her face had lost something of its solid blue-eyed imperturbability; her cheeks had become a trifle concave and her jaw seemed longer. Always Mrs. Wilby had been proud of her clear white complexion, and now her skin had become sallow and dull, with a muddy yellow undertone. Ronald knew that his mother worried far too much about money; she drove herself too hard and worked overtime whenever possible and sometimes late into the night, typing legal documents for one of her acquaintances who was a court-reporter. Ronald wished she'd ease up, relax just a bit. It might take a few months longer before they were ready to move: what of it? He was quite comfortable and making no complaints — except at the food and the studies which often took up three or four hours.

One morning in early May, Ronald heard his mother descend the stairs more slowly than usual, and when she served his breakfast she gave him no instructions regarding his studies, which he thought odd. He lay flat on the floor and peered out through the secret door. "Mother?"

"Yes, Ronald."

"If you're tired, why don't you stay home today and rest?"

"I'd like to, dear, but the work is piled up on me, and I can't take the time off. If Mr. Lang thought I wasn't capable of doing the job, he might hire somebody else, and I'd be out in the street. I'll feel better tonight. I've picked up a bug of some kind, and it's made me a bit unsettled."

"You'd better see the doctor, Mother."

"No, it's nothing. I've taken my pills and I'll be good as new by noon."

A few minutes later she went off to work. Ronald heard the front door close and the diminishing steps as she crossed the porch and descended to the walk. A moment later he detected the grind of the starter, the hum of the engine, and then there was silence.

The day passed. Ronald exercised, worked out a set of the hated algebraic problems, forced himself to read a chapter in the biology text, and prepared the resumé which his mother required. He lunched on peanut butter and jelly sandwiches, reconstituted milk to which he was now inured, and a dish of lemon jello. During the afternoon he napped, then worked on full-length portraits of the six Wizard-Dukes. The costumes were picturesque indeed, each based upon the heraldic colors of the particular duchy. He became engrossed in his work and time went by swiftly; in fact, when he looked at his electric clock he discovered that five o'clock had come: time for his mother to be home, unless she were shopping or otherwise delayed.

At six o'clock he frowned and listened, but heard no sounds, nor did his mother return home at any time during the evening. Ronald sat hunched and worried until eleven o'clock, when in spite of his anxiety, he began to doze.

At nine o'clock the following morning, with no word from his mother, Ronald opened the secret door and after a period of rumination crawled forth.

The day was dark and dreary; rain fell in spasmodic gusts against the windows. Ronald crawled into the living room and hesitantly telephoned the office where his mother worked.

"Central Valley Hardware," said a brisk voice.

Ronald cleared his throat. "Mrs. Wilby, please."

"Mrs. Wilby isn't in today. Do you care to leave a message?"

"This is the pound. It's about her cat. I've called her home and she's not there."

"Mrs. Wilby is sick. She's in the hospital just now, and I don't know when you can get in touch with her."

"Thank you." Ronald hung up the telephone. So: his mother was sick. Again. He thought she had seemed somewhat peaked.

Ronald crawled back into the kitchen, where he sat on the linoleum floor and listened to the rain. The house seemed lonely and distant, not at all cozy. He went to the refrigerator and investigated its contents. Eight eggs, hamburger, half a pound of margarine, carrots, celery, two tomatoes in the crisper, a few oddments of this and that. Crouching out of Mrs. Schumacher's range of vision, Ronald fried the hamburger and four eggs, and sitting on the floor devoured the lot, along with four slices of bread, margarine and peanut butter, with a quart of milk to wash it all down. He had neglected the freezer! Here he discovered a carton half-full of vanilla ice cream which his mother doled out a spoonful or two at a time as a special treat. Ronald opened a can of peaches, which he poured into a bowl and scraped all the ice cream out on top, and this was his dessert. It was the best meal he'd had since his Christmas dinner. Gorged and torpid, Ronald crawled back into his lair, where he lay on his cot wondering how long his mother would be ill. There was little point in doing any algebra until she was on hand to correct the papers; she wouldn't want to come home to a lot of algebra problems. He'd just take a vacation from studies until she returned: certainly the most sensible program.

Four days went by and no word from his mother. Ronald began to dread her homecoming. She'd be sick with frustration over so much money spent on the hospital. It would mean rations even more spartan than before: beans, rice, dry milk, dandelion greens. No peanut butter, no juicy hamburgers, no ice cream, no cakes or pastry. A drab existence indeed. But he had no choice in the matter.

Ronald preferred to cook in his lair, where he could relax. To save himself trouble he moved in a quantity of those provisions he liked the most. The bread was all gone; he ate soda crackers until the package was empty.

On the morning of the sixth day, Ronald heard footsteps on the porch. He jumped up eagerly and put his ear to the plasterboard. The key rattled in the lock, the door opened. He heard a man's voice. "...those were my instructions from Mr. Wilby. He wants to sell as quickly as possible, and whatever furniture and oddments you don't want go to charity."

"I don't think I want a thing except some family photographs," said a woman's voice. "I've got all the furniture I need, and it wouldn't be worth shipping back to Pennsylvania anyway."

"You're right there. It doesn't appear that she had too much. What about the books?"

"I don't think I want them."

"China? Silver? That clock?"

"Yes, I'll take the old clock. It belonged to my father, and Elaine got it as a wedding present when she married Mr. Wilby."

"I'll put it aside. Is there anything else?"

"Let me just look into her room, in case I recognize any family jewelry. But I don't believe there's a thing I want except the photographs."

"Here's a picture. What about this?"

"My word, no. It's her son Ronald. I wouldn't want to be reminded of him an instant. Poor Elaine. She lived a tragic life."

"I'll agree to that. It was cancer, wasn't it?"

"No, it was something rather different. She'd had a gall bladder operation and evidently one of the stones slipped down into the bile duct, affecting the work of her liver."

"My word, think of that! I never knew gall-stones were so dangerous!"

"They are in a case like this, because the person thinks she's cured. Poor Elaine had a terrible attack at work, and before the doctors could help her she'd passed on."

"Far better than a lingering death."

"Yes indeed. I hope I go as fast."

"A pity. She was a comparatively young woman. Well, let's take a look in the bedrooms."

The two climbed the stairs; their footsteps sounded over Ronald's head where he lay stiff and terrified. His mother, his wonderful mother: she was dead! And he was alone, with no one to care for him! His dear mother, who loved him so! Tears sprang to Ronald's eyes; he wanted to wail out his grief; he wanted to pound his head with his fists, cover himself under his blankets. What would he do now? No one to talk to him, or cook his meals, or take care of him. Ronald bit the bedclothes to stifle his sobbing; the man and the woman — evidently his Aunt Margaret — were on their way downstairs.

The two stood in the front hall. The man said: "If that's all you want, you might as well take it now. Tomorrow I'll get the Goodwill truck out here and they can clean everything out."

"Such a funny old house," said Aunt Margaret. "Will anyone buy such a place?"

"You'd be surprised! With four big bedrooms, the big kitchen, dining room and living room? There's lots of people with families who'll find this just what they want."

"It's not my cup of tea. I like things a bit more modern. Oh, just one thing. I'll look at the silver, and maybe..." Ronald heard the dining room drawers being opened. "It's just plate," said Aunt Margaret. "Not worth the bother of carrying back to Pennsylvania."

"I can see your point. Well then, shall we go?"

"Yes. This place gives me the shivers."

The door opened and closed; Ronald heard them descending the front steps. He lay like a statue, his interior congealed and unresponsive. So now — what should he do? Where could he go? He had no money, no food... A truck would be coming tomorrow to take all the familiar old things, and he'd never see them again. Ronald crawled out his secret door and carried all the provisions his mother had bought in Stockton into his lair, and everything else edible he could find in the pantry. At least they couldn't take his food away.

What else would he want to keep? Up in his closet was his good suit and his best shoes. Ronald crawled forth and for the first time since his immurement went up to his room. It was just as he had left it, dear and friendly, but a place unthinkably far, like an old man's dream of his childhood. He examined his trinkets and mementos; they belonged to a world which had included his mother. That world had disappeared; the room had lost its meaning.

He packed a suitcase with clothes and one or two keepsakes he could not bear to leave behind: the Swiss Army knife which his mother had given him on his fourteenth birthday, the teddy bear which had been his first toy. He carried the suitcase and an armload of his favorite books down to his lair, closed the secret door and lay down on his cot to think. Sooner or later, when his food ran out, he'd have to leave. Ronald blinked back tears. The land was broad, the roads were long and led afar, to strange pitiless places Ronald really did not care to visit. He beat the pillow with his fist. "Oh my, oh my!" he half-whispered, half-wailed, "why can't things be like they were? I don't want to leave my home!"

CHAPTER XI

EARLY IN THE MORNING Ronald looked once more about the house for anything he wanted to keep. He considered the television set, but it was too large to fit through his secret door. He brought in all the light bulbs, toilet paper, and paper napkins he could find and a few kitchen implements. He also decided to retain the old toolbox; one never knew when tools might come in handy. There was no room in his lair, so he raised the trap door and took the toolbox down to the crawl-space and hid it in a dark corner.

He went up to his mother's room to look around and was almost trapped. He just happened to glance out the window and saw the Goodwill truck stopping in front of the house. He ran down the stairs, bounded on all fours across the dining room and kitchen and dived into his lair. Down went the secret door; he was secure.

A moment later the front door opened. Footsteps sounded in the front hall. The man who had come yesterday said, "Take everything. Clear the place out. One thing I want to ask you, or rather two things: be careful of the floors, they're in good shape now and I don't want to refinish them, and secondly, don't leave a mess. Clean up as you go."

"We'll do our best, but we're not going to haul off the trash, mister. We're not garbage movers."

"There's not a great deal of trash, if any. And if you can't cooperate with me, don't even start, because I can get somebody here who will."

"No need to get huffy, mister. I just want to state that we're here to move furniture, not tidy up the place."

"Take everything but the television. That's been spoken for elsewhere. I'm going now. Lock up when you're finished."

The real-estate agent planned to take the television for himself, thought Ronald.

The Goodwill men worked until noon. Ronald listened flint-eyed to their comings and goings. Finally the house was silent and Ronald came forth from his lair.

The house was stark and bleak: bare except for the television set. Now that his mother was gone Ronald actually preferred the house in its present condition. But what was he going to do with himself; what was he going to do?

Ronald looked over the television set with sabotage in mind, but the real-estate agent's car stopped in front of the house, and Ronald bounded back to his lair.

The man came and went. Ronald once more emerged; as he had expected the television set was gone.

Ronald sat down on the naked hardwood floor. Afternoon sunlight presently waned; twilight drifted in from the east. Ronald's mind was blank. He no longer felt anxious about the future; there was no future to feel anxious about. When his food ran out he would leave the house by night, hike ten miles to Mileta and hitchhike from there into Berkeley, where he would lose himself among all the other nameless waifs. Eventually—but there was no point probing that far into the mist. Right now he felt as sad and faded as the evening sky. He dozed and woke up in darkness with a shaft of light from the streetlamp glistening on the hardwood floor... Ronald lay quiet, not quite sure where he was. The house seemed very old and whispered with voices too dim to be heard. He was one with these voices; he need fear nothing... He felt stiff and cold and went to his lair.

The next morning Ronald awoke earlier than usual. He lay on his cot painfully conscious of the silence. Never again the brisk thud of his mother's footsteps descending the stairs, or the bustle in the kitchen as she cooked his meals. Ronald's eyes filled with tears.

After a good breakfast he felt better. Life must go on. He had ample paper and colored inks; with no vexing distractions like algebra and history and biology, he could work with far better concentration, and spend as much time as he liked on detail and elaboration.

First he performed his exercises: by now almost a compulsive act; he could not relax until his muscles had been stretched and twisted. Additionally, he had become a bit heavier than he wished to be.

About ten o'clock footsteps sounded on the front porch; the lock clicked and the door opened. Into the house came several people, and one of them was a woman.

Ronald heard a voice he recognized, that of the real-estate agent. "The living room is on your right. As you can see it's got good proportions and nice high ceilings. They didn't stint on space in the days when this house was built."

"Just when was that?" asked a man.

"I'd guess about the turn of the century. It's quite an old house, but absolutely solid and sound. They built well in those days."

"The floors are nice," said a woman. "Does the fireplace smoke?"

"I really couldn't say, Mrs. Putnam. I don't see why it should. The chimney's got a good long rise to get a draught going. We'll start a fire if you like."

"Oh no, don't bother."

"Now over here is the dining room, paneled very nicely in redwood — there's no wood that mellows more beautifully with age. Built-in sideboard, and a nice eastern outlook to catch the morning sunlight. A very cheerful room. If I owned this house I'd invest in a really good chandelier, and this would be a gracious room indeed."

"Yes, very nice," said Mrs. Putnam.

"Out here is the kitchen," said the agent. "Plenty space, lots of room to work, and a convenient pantry, again an item you don't find nowadays."

"The stove doesn't amount to much," said Mrs. Putnam, "and this refrigerator is absolutely antique."

"You'd probably want to modernize a bit," said the agent. "Quite understandable. I'd do so myself, and just between you and me, this is why the price is so attractive. The owner wants to sell. Out here is the utility porch."

"But no downstairs bathroom?"

"No downstairs bathroom. In those days, ha ha, indoor plumbing of any kind was a luxury."

"Well, I don't know about that," said Mr. Putnam. "It doesn't seem too convenient."

"Let's take a look upstairs," said the agent. "Four big bedrooms and a very nice large bathroom: just the house for a large family."

"I don't think we'll bother, Mr. Roscoe. We've only got our one boy, and already he's talking about the army. We'd just rattle around in a house this large."

"Very well. I just thought it might strike your fancy. We don't get these fine old houses on the market too often, and I decided I'd give you first look."

"Thanks very much, Mr. Roscoe, but I think we want something more modern: a ranch-style place with a nice patio."

"I've got some of those I can show you too, and in their price range they're good buys. Just how many..." The closing of the front door cut off Mr. Roscoe's question. Ronald heard them descend the front steps and presently it was quiet again.

Ronald sat scowling. He wanted no one moving into his house, annoying him with their noises, their comings and goings. Nothing he could do to prevent it, of course. Maybe the house wouldn't be sold.

Mr. Roscoe returned about three o'clock with another prospect: a young woman by the lilt of her voice. Ronald wondered what she looked like; she sounded pert and energetic and attractive, and Mr. Roscoe's gallant jocosities confirmed his suspicion. From the conversation Ronald gathered that her husband owned a service station, that she liked the house, but her children were very young, and she was afraid they might fall down the stairs. Mr. Roscoe pooh-poohed the notion, but the young woman was quite definite. Mr. Roscoe quickly took her elsewhere.

Ronald sat musing over the young woman's voice and her possible appearance. What his lair lacked was a vantage or one-way mirror which would allow him to see without being seen. He considered the walls. Perhaps something could be arranged. The built-in sideboard in the dining room backed up against his lair; at the rear of the central alcove was a rather cloudy mirror. Crawling into the dining room Ronald examined the mirror. Not a one-way mirror, of course. But still — well, it was worth a try. He brought his tools up from the crawl-space. First he measured, then broke into the wall of his lair behind the sideboard, removing lath and plaster until the heavy cardboard behind the sideboard mirror was laid bare. Once again he checked his measurements, then cut a hole through the cardboard, to reveal the gray coating at the back of the glass. With great care he scratched away a fragment of the silvering, to reveal clear glass. Aha! Ronald put his eye to the tiny window and was afforded a view across the dining room, very limited, to be sure, but better than no view whatever. The spot was so inconspicuous that Ronald felt justified in removing somewhat more of the silvering, to enlarge his field of vision. When the peephole was not in use, he would cover it with a bit of tinfoil and a cover to prevent any possible leakage of light from his lair, which of course could bring his whole secret world crashing down around his ears, if not worse.

The following day was quiet; Mr. Roscoe failed to appear. Ronald was of two minds about Mr. Roscoe's absence. He resented the intrusions; still and undeniably, the visitors made the day interesting.

The next day Mr. Roscoe made up for his poor showing and brought three different sets of prospects. Ronald, standing by his peephole, examined them as they walked past, but in no case did he approve of what he saw and heard.

On the next day Mr. Roscoe showed the house to a Mrs. Wood, a trim neatly dressed woman of about forty who approved the sheer old-fashioned spaciousness, and the four bedrooms which the size of her family made indispensable. She seemed a pleasant woman, although she vigorously bargained with Mr. Roscoe over the price of the house. Mr. Roscoe was smilingly firm. "I can't relax a dollar's worth. The owner gave me his first, last and final figure, and the only leeway I have is my commission, which naturally I want to keep. I assure you, the price is right. You won't get this much house anywhere in Oakmead for the money, believe me. I know, I'm in the business."

"The house has possibilities," said Mrs. Wood, "and with my three girls I need the bedrooms…The kitchen is pretty bad, you'll admit. In fact, everything needs a good coat of paint. Still, the floors are beautiful, and I do like the feeling of space."

"They don't build them like this nowadays."

"Well, I'll talk to my husband. We've looked at five or six houses already and they're either too small or too expensive or both. The price here seems high to me, no matter what you say. The house isn't all that convenient and it needs redecoration."

Mr. Roscoe shrugged. "I'm sorry, Mrs. Wood. My hands are tied. I can't do a thing."

"Well, we'll just keep looking."

Two hours later Mr. Roscoe was back with a stout middle-aged couple whom he addressed as Mr. and Mrs. Florio. Mr. Florio, who was chubby and somewhat pompous, declared the house to be exactly what they were looking for. "A nice old-fashioned place, quiet neighborhood, low taxes — what more do we want? Look at that nice wood in the dining room."

"Yes, it's nice," said Mrs. Florio. "I like all the room, but there's lots of things wrong only a lady would see. The kitchen needs a new stove and a new sink. We could use our own refrigerator and give that old monster away. There's not good storage downstairs except for the pantry which is nice. And think of running up the stairs every time you wanted to go to the toilet."

"Oh well, maybe we could remodel that back porch, put in a little toilet out there. And there's nothing wrong with that stove. It heats up, don't it?"

"It doesn't suit me. Do you think I'd want to show my kitchen to Rosa and Mary and Mrs. Vargas with things in it like this?"

"Well, maybe we could fix it all up. What's money?"

"What's money, you say. Until I ask you to spend some."

"Well, listen, it wouldn't cost all that much, I'm telling you! Two, three thousand maybe."

"And you'd have a very nice house," said Mr. Roscoe approvingly.

"Well, we'll talk about it," said Mrs. Florio, and there the matter rested.

The next prospect was a divorced lady, Mrs. Cindy Turpin, only recently arrived in Oakmead. "Do you know, I just love the look of this place! It's pure San Francisco: you've seen them, all those beautiful old white houses with the bay windows!"

"I know what you mean," said Mr. Roscoe. "They're very attractive."

"I was brought up in a house like this, on Russian Hill, and I know my little ones would love this place just as much. We're all folk-dancers and there'd be ever so much room just to swing and strut!"

"You have a very talented family! How old are the children?"

"Well, Jacob is fourteen, Cornelia is twelve, Todd is ten, and Guinevere is eight: all just two years apart. They're so cute in their costumes! I play the guitar, of course."

"It's a beautiful family. And there's plenty of room for them here."

"There certainly is! I'll have to bring Jeff—that's my ex-husband— here to see it. He's buying the place for me."

"You'd better hurry, because I've got several other people interested. There's not many old San Francisco-type houses like this on the market."

"Oh, I know! I'll call him tonight!"

They stood in the dining room; Ronald watched through the mirror. Mrs. Turpin was a nervously active woman, long-legged and long-armed, with a round big-featured face and large wet eyes. Ronald frowned. They'd be making a lot of noise and bothering him with their prancing around. Still—hmm. Ronald licked his lips; it might be interesting.

On the next three days, Mr. Roscoe brought five different parties, including a Negro family, which infected Ronald with a furious hatred toward Mr. Roscoe. Is this what he wanted to do with the house where a decent family had spent all their lives? He wondered if Mr. Roscoe would sell the house next to his own to Negroes!

The Negroes, Mr. and Mrs. Wayne, like most of the other prospective buyers, had a large family. Ronald by now was a keen judge of real-estate selling and sales resistance. He had decided that the more a person admired this and that, the less likely that person was to buy, inasmuch as enthusiasm could not help but firm the asking price, which everyone asserted to be unreasonable.

Abruptly the tours of the house came to an end. A week passed without a sign of either Mr. Roscoe or any of his prospects. Then one day a termite inspector appeared. He examined the periphery of the house, probed here and there with an ice pick, roamed the crawl-space conducting further investigations. Ronald wondered what the visit portended. Perhaps the house had been sold?

The same day Ronald made a careful survey of the living room. His peephole into the dining room had provided a good deal of edification; he wondered if possibly a similar arrangement could be effected through the opposite wall into the living room. At first glance the situation lacked promise. The stairs obstructed all but that section where the toilet was situated, and the wall in the living room lacked a mirror. However, six feet above the living room floor, an ornate plate rack, for the display of trinkets, plaques, dishes and bric-a-brac, encircled the room. Ronald calculated that by prying down the molding underneath the plate rack he could create a suitable crack. In the event that someone noticed the crack they would merely assume that the wood had shrunk, or a nail had given way.

Once more Ronald brought up his tools and presently produced so excellent a view that he crawled quickly around to the living room, spraddling like an enormous four-legged crab, in order to check the appearance of the crack. But all was in order: the crack, from this side, ran in the shadow of the overhanging ledge and was well camouflaged. To cover both of the peepholes when his light was on, Ronald contrived secure masks. A single lapse would spell disaster! He could afford no fit of absentmindedness!

On the following day a tall thin man with clear blue eyes, a mild good-natured face, grizzled brown hair worn in a rather scruffy crew cut, arrived at the house. Ronald inspected him through the living room peephole. The man's gray suit, blue-and-white striped shirt, and nondescript tie conveyed an indefinable sense of officialdom; Ronald thought that he must be a city employee, or a representative of the PG&E, come to check something about the house. A detective? Ronald's heart rose in his throat. Had someone seen him as he moved about the house? Ronald slowly relaxed. A man so vague and casual would hardly be a policeman.

The man paced slowly back and forth in the living room. Ten minutes passed, then another car drew up outside. The man went to the front door, threw it open, and in came three teenage girls, followed by the calm efficient woman Ronald remembered from a week or two previously. Mrs. Wood was her name; she was the lady who had haggled so insistently with Mr. Roscoe, and the man was evidently her husband.

"Well, here we are," Mrs. Wood said gaily. "Have you been waiting long?"

"Just a few minutes," said Mr. Wood. He asked the girls, "How do you like it?"

"Well — it's better than the other places," said the oldest girl. "But isn't it a bit dreary?" Ronald, watching through the peephole, put her age at about seventeen.

"I know what you mean!" said the second, who was about fifteen. "There's an atmosphere here!"

The youngest, aged about twelve or thirteen, wrinkled her nose. "It's not an atmosphere. It's just a funny smell, like old clothes, or something dead."

"That's just mustiness," said Mrs. Wood. "It'll go away as soon as we open the windows. Have you looked over the bedrooms?"

"Not yet." The girls ran up the stairs and Ronald heard them chattering as they prowled the upper floor. Bad smell indeed! That wasn't a nice thing to say. Smart-aleck girls, spoiled rotten all three of them. But he could hardly wait till they returned downstairs, because all three were extraordinarily pretty. Ronald moved back and forth between his peepholes, tense with excitement, while Mr. and Mrs. Wood wandered here and there, discussing various aspects of the house. Ronald gathered that Mr. Roscoe had telephoned the night before, announcing that the owner had reduced his price, and were they still interested?

The girls came back downstairs. "Well," said Mr. Wood, "what do you think?"

"It's okay," said the youngest, who was gay and cute and giddy. A real show-off! thought Ronald. "At least we'd all have bedrooms."

The oldest, who was quiet and mild and, like her father, rather vague, said: "We could paint the house, and make it a lot more cheerful."

"It's a challenge," said the middle girl, who seemed the most intense and perhaps the most intelligent. "No doubt about that."

Mrs. Wood said, "The place looks bleak just now. All empty houses do. Once we brought in our furniture and put down our rugs and hung up new drapes, there'd be a big difference."

"I wish we could get rid of that old stove. It's kind of icky," said the youngest girl, whose name seemed to be Babs or Bobby.

"We'll have to look at the budget and see how much it'll stand," said Mr. Wood. "But I think we could plan on a new stove and a new refrigerator."

"Then we're agreed," said Mrs. Wood, the most decisive. "We'll take the house."

"It's not a bad investment," said Mr. Wood. "If we redecorate and put in a lawn, we can always get our money back."

"Sometime we should convert that back porch to a bathroom," said Mrs. Wood briskly.

"Oh Daddy!" cried Althea, the second girl, "let's go down to the store right now and buy some paint and a stove and a new refrigerator!"

"Not so fast," said Mrs. Wood. "First we've got to make sure of the house. There'll be plenty to do, don't worry about that."

"Have you decided who gets which bedroom?" Mr. Wood asked the girls, half-smiling for their excitement and the fun they were having.

"No, not yet. We haven't talked about it."

"You can draw straws or something of the sort," Mrs. Wood suggested.

"Oh, we'll let Ellen have the front room," said Althea. "Babs can have whichever of the back rooms she wants. It makes no difference to me."

Mr. Wood held out his closed hands. "Whoever gets the hand with the penny gets the room to the right of the hall."

Babs touched her father's left hand and found the penny, and thus the bedrooms were allotted.

Evening had come. The Woods had departed and the house was quiet. Ronald came forth from his lair and crawled into the living room. It was no longer the living room he knew so well; it was no longer the same house. The Woods now lived here: Mr. Benjamin Wood, Mrs. Marcia Wood, Ellen, Althea and Barbara Wood.

Ronald spent quite some time thinking about the girls. All were charming, each in her personal and distinctive way. Barbara was blonde and cute, with a snub nose, a pretty pink mouth. In every blonde girl Ronald looked for traces of Laurel Hansen, and in Barbara he thought to discern certain of Laurel's flirtatious habits. Barbara was extremely self-assured and full of merry pranks, as befitted the spoiled youngest daughter of the family.

Althea, the second daughter, was an inch taller than Barbara, and rather slender, with fine blonde-brown hair flowing to her shoulders; she seemed more moody and introspective, and perhaps more imaginative, than either Barbara or Ellen. Althea's cheeks were flat, her jaw was delicate; when she mused, her mouth drooped, and she seemed as forlorn as a wind-fairy. A girl of interesting attributes, thought Ronald.

Ellen, the oldest girl, was again a person unique and distinctive, although she lacked a definite style, like Babs' extravagant foolishness and Althea's dreamy-wry romantic quality. Ellen was merely beautiful. She exhibited a most curious quality of radiance. Her hair, fine brown-gold like Althea's, seemed to glow of itself; her eyes were transparent gray; her skin, golden from the sunlight, seemed to luminesce with health and cleanliness.

The three girls complemented each other. Each seemed to approve and enjoy the special qualities of the other two; each took pleasure in fulfilling her own role. Babs was the cute 'spoiled brat'; she was supposed to be reckless, saucy and flamboyant, though she was not really any of these; it was all an amusing, affectionate game, played with equal zest by all the sisters. Similarly, Althea was the poet, the dreamer, the source of odd ideas, while Ellen was the innocent impractical sister who overflowed with love and generosity.

Three days later the Woods took up residence at 572 Orchard Street, and tranquility fled out the window. Turmoil was the new way of life as the Woods worked to alter the austere personality of the old house. Ronald's privacy became a thing of the past. Inconsequential conversations intruded upon his thoughts. He could no longer sleep, eat, or flush the toilet as he wished, but must wait upon the convenience of the newcomers.

Ronald was not only irritated; he was enthralled and fascinated. He could not get enough of the girls; they tantalized him with their comings and more with their goings, and their most interesting activities always occurred beyond his range of vision. If only he were able to open peepholes into their bedrooms!

In spite of his annoyance, Ronald became interested in the affairs of the Woods. He had no real choice; they surrounded him; their topics and concerns pervaded the air.

Ronald soon acquired background information regarding the Woods. Ben Wood worked for the telephone company, and had done so since leaving the army — a period of twenty years. He had been transferred to Oakmead from Los Gatos, a town halfway between San Francisco and Monterey. No one had wanted to make the move, but Ben Wood could not afford to pass up the promotion involved. Ellen and Althea would attend Oakmead High in the fall. Barbara would enter the ninth grade at junior high. No one in the family liked Oakmead very much, and they had bought the house at 572 Orchard only because it was cheap and roomy and could be made at least tolerable by dint of hard work and enthusiasm, which everyone was prepared to expend. Ronald became a passive participant in the project; again, he had no choice. The house and its refurbishing were almost the only topics of conversation. First there was cleaning, then scraping and painting, and likewise planting. Ben Wood blasted the family budget with a new stove, dishwasher, refrigerator, a washer and a dryer. He installed new kitchen cabinets, laid down new tile in the kitchen, removed the old washtubs from the back porch and wrecked the old shed at the back of the lot, and who should he hire to haul away the junk but Duane Mathews? He rented a cultivator, tilled the back yard. The girls set out a vegetable garden; Marcia Wood planted fruit trees and rose bushes; Ben Wood installed a new front lawn, which he declared would make the Schumacher lawn look sick, and the challenge somehow communicated itself to the Schumachers, who began to water and mow and clip more diligently than ever.

The outside of the house remained as before: chalk-white, the color of sun-bleached bone. Next year the Woods planned to repaint the house a dark green with white trim.

The work occupied the family most of the summer, but they did not lack for help. While hauling away the rubbish, Duane Mathews became acquainted with Ellen, and thereafter was almost a daily participant in the work. Various other boys came more or less regularly to lend their efforts. Mrs. Wood provided hamburgers and lemonade, and the girls wore shorts, which seemed sufficient inducement. "The more the merrier," said Ben Wood, "so long as they work."

"They work," said Marcia Wood. "The girls won't let them stop."

"Merciless little slave drivers."

In spite of himself Ronald became interested in the summer's work. With the assiduity of a scientist he kept watch at the peepholes. The girls aroused his special interest; their smooth brown legs and round little rumps were sources of sweet torment. Ronald, with his eye glued to the peephole, was never satiated. When one of the girls walked past his hands would grow moist, and he would make soft noises under his breath. He had no favorites, and appreciated the different quality of each girl. If he had been asked to make a choice he would have considered long before selecting, though he had formed quite definite opinions as to their special qualities. Barbara was the cutest and most seductive; Ellen was the most beautiful and perhaps the most passionate; while Althea's dreamy personality gave her a strange charm which Ronald found irresistible. For the boys who came to visit and perhaps to work he felt nothing but dislike and contempt, and most especially for Duane Mathews, who had fallen in love with Ellen.

One Sunday at lunchtime Duane mentioned horrid Ronald Wilby, the murderer. The Woods were shocked by the news. "I thought there was an evil atmosphere about this house!" said Althea in an awed voice. "I felt it when we first moved in. It was so strong you could almost smell it!"

"It's gone now, though," said Barbara. "Wickedness can't stand being painted."

"Don't be too sure!" Steve Mullins told her. "You've heard of evil influences? If they're strong enough they form into ghosts."

"Oh? And how do you know?" Ellen asked.

"Where else do you think ghosts come from?"

"I don't even know if there are such things."

"A lot of people swear they've seen them."

"A lot more swear they haven't."

"Even so," said Barbara, "the ghost wouldn't be here. It would haunt that old garden."

"Don't say that!" muttered Duane Mathews. "It was my little sister!"

"I'm sorry!" cried Barbara. "I didn't mean to say anything awful."

Duane managed a grim laugh. "That's all right. I shouldn't be all hung up on it. Maybe someday I'll find Ronald Wilby."

Seven feet away Ronald Wilby stood with his eye pressed to the peephole. More than anyone he knew he abhorred Duane Mathews, an ugly graceless fellow whose father was a bartender. How Ellen or anyone else could like a person so eaten up with malice exceeded Ronald's comprehension. Every aspect of Duane's appearance and personality repelled Ronald: his harsh bony features, his lanky body, all shoulders, arms and legs; his abrupt motions and terse, brusque voice. And most of all, his practicality and grim self-assurance, which in Ronald's mind were equivalent to arrogance and bloated egotism. Only a year or two older than Ronald, Duane had the presumption to act like a man! And in spite of all, the girls seemed to admire him. Only yesterday Ronald had heard them chattering about Duane in the usual half-foolish, half-mordant hyperboles which none but themselves could fully understand.

"He looks like an old-fashioned cowboy," Barbara had said. "From Texas, of course."

"He even acts old-fashioned," said Althea. "He's somebody out of an old movie."

"An old cowboy movie."

"Whatever you like. Tickets cost the same."

"His eyes are marvelous," sighed Ellen. "I wish I had sea-green eyes."

Snake's eyes, thought Ronald. Carol, so he recalled, also had odd green eyes.

"I'll have to look in my book of astral psychology and see what sea-green eyes mean," said Althea. "It might be something awful, and then we'd have to turn poor Duane away."

"Mom likes him, eyes and all," said Barbara. "That tells us more about who gets turned away around here than any old book with a purple cover."

"Then I'll look in my book on palmistry with the red cover."

"About Duane's eyes?"

"No, his hands."

"But he doesn't have green hands."

Althea liked to use a voice with a special cool twang when she propounded a paradox. "Duane has serious faults. He's too dependable and trustworthy. Around people like Duane a girl can relax and sometimes she falls asleep."

Ellen smiled sadly. "Only cads keep you awake?"

"Around cads I *stay* awake," said Althea. "But don't get me wrong. I'm not a bigot. Some of my best friends are cads." She thrust up her hands as Barbara started to speak. "Don't you dare say it."

Such had been the conversation of yesterday morning. Today Duane looked quizzical when Althea addressed him as "Tex", though, characteristically, he forebore to ask why the nickname.

After lunch the five went upstairs to paint the front bedroom: Ellen, Althea, Barbara, Duane, and Steve Mullins, who was one among the many enamored of Barbara and her outrageous antics. Ronald could hear their voices, and they seemed to be having a good time.

Ronald closed the peepholes, turned on his light, and went to sit on the cot. The conversation, specifically that part dealing with himself, had soured the day. He felt cantankerous and dissatisfied, and in no mood for any of his usual activities... Not but what his ordinary routines hadn't already been disturbed. Ronald sighed and growled. He just couldn't let those twerps interfere with his activities. He rose from the couch and put himself through a lackadaisical set of exercises, though nowadays he dared no jogging unless everyone was gone from the house.

As always, exercising gave him an appetite. For his dinner, Ronald opened a can of beans which he ate with the last of his soda crackers smeared with peanut butter, a rather bland meal which left Ronald's appetite unappeased, especially when, for Sunday dinner, Mrs. Wood served mushroom soup, avocado salad, a beautiful pineapple-glazed ham with sweet potatoes and fresh green broccoli. Ronald glumly watched through the peephole as the five Woods devoured their dinner. Everyone was cheerful; the interior of the house was now completely painted except for trim around the doors and windows, which would require enamel. As Marcia Wood had originally prophesied, fresh paint had gone far to enliven the old house, and everyone enjoyed the spaciousness of the big old Victorian rooms.

"If we added on some turrets and balconies, and bought a few marble urns, we could call the place a mansion," said Ellen.

"A Gothic mansion," said Althea. "That's what they're called in the horror movies."

"The remark is too close for comfort," said Barbara. "The last people to live here were definitely spooky. I doubt if they left any ghosts, however. At least I hope not."

"I share your hope," said Ben Wood. "Because down would go the market value."

"Maybe that's why the house was sold so cheap."

"We could always advertise in spiritualist magazines," said Althea. "A good dependable ghost might be valuable."

"What good is money," asked Barbara, "if we're all found dead in our beds with horrible expressions on our faces?"

"Barbara, you're being absurd, as usual."

Ellen grimaced. "I wouldn't take you seriously, except that the house *does* have an uncanny feeling about it."

"Bah," said Marcia Wood. "That's just ridiculous."

"Sometimes I hear funny noises," said Barbara. "I suppose it's rats."

"All old houses are full of funny noises," said Ben Wood.

"If you say so, Daddy."

Ronald was displeased by the tenor of the conversation. Certain of the remarks verged on the personal, and why in the world couldn't they stop harping about that old subject? They really had no right to criticize when they only knew Duane's side of the story...Well, it didn't make all that much difference. Of more immediate interest was that lovely ham and the platter of sweet potatoes. Ronald was hungry all over again. The lair had its advantages and also disadvantages, such as watching other people devouring savory meals to which he had not been invited.

For dessert Mrs. Wood served a magnificent lemon meringue pie, and Ronald became almost sick with longing. After this he wouldn't watch the Woods at their meals; he only tortured himself...Ha! Ronald dismissed the idea immediately; it was quite unrealistic.

The girls discussed colors and interior decorating. Ellen had painted her room white, with pale green and lavender trim. Althea had used gray, pale blue and dark blue with accents of white. Barbara had ranged the length and breadth of the sample chip rack in the paint store, to achieve what she called 'drama'. "I want lots of excitement in my room!" she declared, and Ronald muttered under his breath, "I'll give you excitement in your room, no fear of that!" Barbara, the youngest of the girls, impressed Ronald as the sexiest, because of her provocative antics, her flirtatious pouts and poses. He had never seen anyone so boy-crazy! Barbara had painted her room white, yellow, chalky blue and pistachio green, with accents of firehouse red and dark blue, and somehow, after arranging her possessions and hanging her posters, she achieved exactly that atmosphere of exuberant frivolity she intended.

Halfway through August Project Redecoration at 572 Orchard Street came to an end, somewhat to the bewilderment of the Woods, who had started to think of scouring, sanding, and painting as a permanent way of life.

Every room in the house had been refurbished. The living room, originally salmon-beige with dark varnished woodwork, had become off-white with a pale blue ceiling. The woodwork was enameled white, as were the bricks of the fireplace, and a bright-blue rug covered the floor.

Ronald disapproved of the changes. The house had previously seemed adequate; the zeal expended by the Wood family represented a not-too-subtle derogation of himself and his mother. The Woods were just plain finicky, thought Ronald, and pretentious to boot. A chandelier in the front hall! Art prints all the way up the stairs! The eccentric new clock on the kitchen wall with hands three feet long! The Mexican *ollas* planted with geraniums on the front porch! All vanity and ostentation! Still — it made no great difference, one way or the other. The place no longer meant anything to him; they could turn it into a Chinese joss house for all he cared.

Ronald's food supplies had dwindled to the danger point; and he had started to derive items of sustenance from the Woods' refrigerator, bread box and fruit bowl. In the small hours of the night he would sally forth for his meal: a morsel here, a bite there, an apple or an orange, perhaps a slice of bread, a lump of cheese, a swallow or two of wonderful nonsynthetic milk! And occasionally when there was an ample leftover dessert, Ronald would treat himself to an inconspicuous portion, and never had food tasted so good!

Always he waited until the house was dark and still. Then out the secret door, through the pantry, into the kitchen: silent as a wraith, so that not even the floor creaked! Then across to the refrigerator, to ease open the door and there! glowing in the pale light like gems on black velvet, the delicious fragments of food from the meal to which he had been a witness some six hours previously. He knew he must be extremely discreet, but sometimes oh! what an effort to restrain himself from gobbling the contents of the refrigerator. And once he heard Mrs. Wood call out in puzzlement, "How strange! I would have sworn I put away seven of those deviled eggs. Now there's only five. Did one of you girls get at them?"

"Not I." "Not I." "Not I."

"I'm going crazy then," said Mrs. Wood. "I remember so distinctly… Maybe your father ate them last night."

The mystery of the missing deviled eggs slipped from her mind, and she did not think to question Ben Wood when he arrived home from work. But that evening, when Ellen placed half a deviled egg on each salad plate, Babs said to her father, "Mom thinks she's going crazy, unless you ate two deviled eggs last night."

Ben Wood stared blankly, then said, "I'll agree to anything if it means preserving your mother's sanity."

"Oho!" cried Babs. "So you're the guilty egg-eater!"

"Will your mother go insane if I deny it?"

"Not quite," said Marcia Wood. "It's just that I thought I put seven eggs away, and this morning I could find only five."

"Rats," said Babs.

"Or ants," suggested Ellen.

"Or ghosts," Althea murmured.

"Now you're being silly," said Marcia Wood. "Obviously I counted wrong." A sudden thought struck her. She looked at Ellen. "Wasn't Duane here last night?"

"No. The night before last."

"My mind really is going," said Marcia Wood. "He's in and out so often that I can't keep track of him."

Ben Wood hated to think of his girls growing up. He spoke in a grumbling voice, "That's the price we pay for all this pulchritude: we have to feed every good-time daddy in town. Sometimes I wonder whether it's love or hunger which brings them around."

"Now Daddy, that's not fair," said Ellen. "Duane has worked very hard around here. Don't forget who carted away all the rubbish, and also who brought over all that venison and the catfish and the apricots, and who pushed the car to get it started, and who put the flashing around the chimney, and who..."

"Stop, stop!" cried Ben Wood. "Duane is the best of the lot, in fact he's indispensable. In fact I better go and let Duane move in."

"Where would he sleep?" asked Barbara innocently. "With Mom?"

"He's an extremely nice boy," said Marcia Wood. "If only he weren't so intense! It makes me nervous sometimes just to be in the same room with him."

"You'd be intense too if a fiend murdered your little sister," declared Babs, and behind the peephole Ronald pursed his lips.

"I'm glad it's Ellen who's got the fiend's bedroom and not me," said Althea.

Ellen made a wry face. "I think I'll trade with Babs."

"Oh no you don't. I've got my room just the way I want it."

"The house is very old," said Ben Wood. "Dozens of fiends may have lived here and slept in all the bedrooms."

"I don't think I'll watch any more horror films," said Babs. "I'm starting to believe all those things."

"Nonsense," scoffed Mrs. Wood. "The film people just rig up those effects to scare silly little girls."

"Oh I know that, but where do they get the ideas to begin with? Nobody invents things out of thin air."

"I'll believe the supernatural when I see it," said Ben Wood. "Weird things always happen to other people."

"I'm not so sure about that," said Althea. "What could be more weird than the missing deviled eggs?"

In his lair Ronald made a set of wincing grimaces. He disliked all allusions to himself or to his activities. "I hate to explode your mystery," said Mrs. Wood, "but it's all coming back to me: there were only five eggs after all."

Ronald grinned to himself. The eggs had been extremely tasty. But never should he take articles of food which might have been counted.

※

The flurry over the missing eggs disturbed Ronald to such an extent that he kept to his lair for two nights. When at last he came forth he took only two slices of bread, a small quantity of butter, a slice off a meat loaf, two cherry tomatoes, and a sprig of parsley. The fruit bowl held four ripening avocados: how he loved avocados! Forbidden fruit! He passed them by with only a longing glance.

Back in his lair he ate the sandwich and the meager salad, and gulped down a glass of reconstituted milk. Everything tasted so good that he wanted to go out for a second helping, and perhaps select the ripest of the avocados. Chances were no one would notice...Remember the deviled eggs? He must learn to control his appetite. All very well, but he also must contrive a way to secure food, because his stocks were just about depleted. Well, he knew what he'd have to do: simply change his method of operations. Heretofore he had taken morsels left over from the evening meal, and he would continue to do so when conditions warranted, but to minimize risk, he must henceforth procure mostly raw materials: a potato, an onion, a cupful of flour, an egg, a slice or two of bacon. If he implemented his plan with judgment and discretion, he should be able to maintain himself adequately and with no one the wiser: a triumph of cool resourcefulness over adversity! For best efficiency he must forage to a definite schedule, that he might not take so much of any one item that its absence would be noticed. A good idea to maintain a record of his acquisitions, or even better, to plot the flow on a chart. Ronald nodded with thoughtful approval. He began to feel that he had achieved a certain self-sufficiency. His mother had often emphasized that planning and foresight distinguished successful men from failures. Ronald now understood the wisdom of her remarks.

First Ronald made sketches to determine the scale and scope of his chart, then drafted it neatly on a large sheet of drawing paper. He would employ different colored inks for the various components of his diet and thus provide instant and accurate information as to what might be called his 'income'. A corollary of this idea occurred to him: he could prepare a second chart to record his consumption, or 'expenditure', and even a third chart to show the level of supplies on hand, or 'inventory'. These charts would then provide a great deal of interesting information, and rationalize what was otherwise a hit-and-miss sort of procedure; he was sure his mother would have approved his methods.

Ronald's new system proved fairly successful. At a glance he could determine his supply of any commodity, and how recently he had commandeered a quantity of this substance; the charts were time-consuming of course, but any worthwhile achievement entailed hard work, which was another of his mother's dictums. The charts helped him formulate a number of guidelines or precepts, the most important of which were:

- *Never take food from a full or nearly full or a nearly empty container.*
- *Take very small quantities of expensive items.*
- *Take no canned goods unless they have been pushed to the back of the shelves and forgotten.*

Ronald's new way of life entailed more effort than the old. He was now obliged to cook: soups, stews, pancakes which he flavored with cheese, jelly, or peanut butter, and cooking was also more of a problem, since he must be careful with cooking odors, and prepare his meals only when any vagrant whiff of this or that would not be noticed: after the Woods had all gone to bed, or while Mrs. Wood herself was cooking. Ronald hung the charts in a neat row on the wall behind the toilet, just under the living room peephole: the only area of wall space not yet dedicated to Atranta. They made an imposing array, and testified to his remarkable and dispassionate logic toward problems which might have confounded an ordinary person. It was clear, thought Ronald, that he combined within himself a pair (at least) of contrasting yet compatible temperaments. To a philosopher's rationality he melded the artist's powers of synthesis; very few people enjoyed this capability!

Perhaps in connection with the Wood family, he should use a more scholarly approach: a spirit of research, so to speak. His situation afforded him a splendid vantage from which to study the activities of a typical contemporary family. He could observe them in a most intimate and detailed manner, like a scientist peering into a terrarium. He could investigate the Woods as an anthropologist examines an exotic tribe; he could codify their activities, the phases of their behavior, their inter-relationships and eccentricities. Someday he might even write a book — a perceptive treatise to amaze the layman and the professional sociologist alike! And how deliriously amusing if the Woods someday should chance upon this book (to be entitled *The Watcher Within,* or *Out of the Secret Place,* or *An Intimate Investigation,* by Ronald Norbert), and marvel to recognize themselves!

Ronald decided to initiate his study at once. Every trifle of knowledge must be organized, every word noted, every gesture analyzed for its symbolic content. He would chart moods and relationships; he would explore hidden currents of pride and envy; he would uncover secrets of which not even other members of the family were aware! The three girls: exuberant Babs, dreamy Althea, luminous Ellen, were the principal topics to which he would address himself. He would learn their likes and dislikes, their foibles and prejudices, their fears and sensitivities; he would know them better than they knew themselves, through his keen and impersonal analysis! Well, not altogether 'impersonal'. Research was all very well, but even better would be a personal study of any or all of the three: separately, all at once, upside-down, or any other way. And Ronald uttered a lewd chuckle, a soft *heh-heh-heh.* Yes, indeed! Yes, sir, indeed!

Chapter XII

Ronald's new project occupied his thoughts the whole of the following day, a Saturday, but a factor he had overlooked came to complicate the situation. On Sunday the summer vacation ended; on Monday the schools opened and all three girls would be spending half their waking hours away from home: a situation which aroused Ronald's bitter resentment. All summer they had given their time to the house and, by some incalculable transference, to Ronald himself; now they would be off and away, living, laughing, feeling, adventuring, far beyond his ken; and to compound the offense, they looked forward to the prospect with anticipation. On Sunday night Ronald wept for self-pity and rage. The girls, so callous, so pitiless, were the agents of his anguish; they must be held to account, and they must suffer as he now suffered: a retribution, perhaps irrational, but Ronald did not care; nothing else could ever allay his hurt. Ronald lay in the dark musing. Which of the girls appealed to him the most? Babs, for her gaiety, for her possibly innocent provocations? Althea, a trifle strange and exotic, who would certainly be entranced with the Atranta saga? Or Ellen, for her glowing beauty?

Gloomy Monday, the first day of school. Ronald sulked all day in the unnaturally quiet house. When the girls returned late in the afternoon, Ronald was so put out that he refused to go to his peepholes. Let them do as they wished! It was all the same to him; he would remove himself into a mood of austere dignity and withdraw his attention, and maybe not even continue his researches.

But at dinner time his hurt feelings succumbed to curiosity, and he applied his eye to the peephole. After apprising himself of the day's events he felt somewhat better, because none of the girls liked their new schools. Barbara found her classmates uninteresting; the girls were either drab, weird, or stuck-up, and the boys were just children. Althea described her teachers as dreary old educational hacks. Ellen expressed a more temperate version of Barbara's views.

Ben and Marcia listened with amusement rather than concern. "You'll soon find people you like," said Ben. "I didn't notice any lack of boys around the house during the summer."

"Yes, but what kind of boys?" grumbled Barbara. "That little jerk Jeff... Fat Peter... Steve Mullins..."

"I thought you liked Steve," said Ben Wood.

Barbara shrugged. "I can get along without him."

"Well, I wouldn't worry too much," said Marcia Wood. "None of you have ever lacked for friends before. I doubt if you will now."

Ellen gave a wry laugh. "I heard one of the girls say, 'They're living in the old Wilby house'... as if that was something to be ashamed of."

"I wouldn't let that kind of nonsense worry me."

"We're certainly not going to move," said Ben Wood. "You can depend on that."

"That's just like the people in this town!" Barbara declared indignantly. "This is our house now, our very own, and we don't care what anybody thinks!"

"If only the house were less, well, 'Gothic'," Althea mused. "It's not really a pretty house."

"Oh come now," said Ben Wood, almost sharply. "It's a very pleasant old house. When it gets a coat of 'Hunter Green' and the trees grow and the garden blooms, it'll be a showplace."

"Allie is far too sensitive to atmospheres," said Ellen.

"If she doesn't look out, she's going to grow up to be a psychiatrist," said Barbara, who often held this particular trade up to scorn.

"I can't help it," said Althea. "Sometimes the house seems alive. Haven't you noticed, when you're coming up the street, how the windows seem to watch you?"

"All houses have faces," said Barbara. "I've seen crying houses and laughing houses, and houses squinting cockeyed, like they're angry —"

"As if they're angry," said Marcia Wood.

"— and remember the old Ettinger house with the cypresses in front? It always looked like, I mean, as if it were praying."

"That's because the Ettingers were Holy Rollers," said Ellen. "A house always begins to look like the people who live there."

"So long as people don't begin to look like their houses," said Althea.

Barbara giggled. "Imagine Daddy with front steps on his stomach and Ellen with gray shingles instead of hair."

"And you painted dark green, as this house is going to be painted next year!"

Marcia Wood changed the subject. "What about activities? Have any of you signed up for anything?"

"No sign-ups till Thursday," said Ellen, "but I don't think I'm interested. It may seem strange, but I'm already thinking about college."

"Oh no!" cried Barbara. "You'll be going away, probably to Berkeley, where there's nothing but hippies and maybe you'll marry one and go off to Turkey or India."

"Not likely," said Ellen. "I might not go to Berkeley. I'd like to go to India though."

"Berkeley's closer," said Althea. "We'd see you more often."

"We should never separate," said Barbara. "Let's promise never to move, but always live with Daddy and Mom. If anybody wants to marry us they've got to move in too."

"Ho ho!" exclaimed Ben Wood. "I hate to think of the grocery bills. I'd have to take two extra jobs."

"Just the same," said Marcia, "it's a lovely idea. I wish we could have it that way… Speaking of extra jobs, I'm tempted to work part-time at the hospital."

"Oh! we don't want you off working!"

"It would just be part-time — maybe mornings, or afternoons, or a day or two a week, to bring a little extra money into the house. Our grocery bills just won't stop, and I refuse to serve spaghetti five nights a week and hamburger the next two. We're just lucky none of you girls have ever needed orthodontia."

"For heaven's sake," said Ben Wood, "please don't anyone do anything that's going to cost money!"

Ronald, grinning to himself, thought, "I'd like to get them all pregnant. Then old Wood could yell about expense!"

But how could the project be accomplished?

Mrs. Wood worked Tuesday and Thursday, and sometimes Wednesday as well. On these days Ronald was alone in the house. The girls' dislike for their schools relieved Ronald's hurt feelings, and he went about his research with gusto.

Not until Thursday, the third day of Mrs. Wood's employment, did Ronald dare to venture from his lair. Cautiously he peered through his secret door and listened, then crawled out into the pantry and rose to his feet. He stepped forth into the kitchen and sniffed the air, detecting new paint, waxed vinyl, freshly laundered curtains, oranges and bananas in the fruit bowl. New curtains of red and green chintz hung at the windows, obscuring Mrs. Schumacher's view. A decided improvement, thought Ronald.

Ronald stood motionless for two minutes, listening and looking all about him, and thrilling to the sense of adventure. He went to the refrigerator and eased it open just to check on what might be there. He decided that he deserved a nice snack. Bringing out milk and ice cream, he mixed a generous quantity of both into a bowl, added sugar, a sliced banana, and a great mound of pressurized whipped cream. With the refined discrimination of an epicure, he devoured his mid-morning snack, sighing in gratification. When he had finished, he washed the bowl and spoons, disposed of the banana peel, and made sure all was as before, though in this easy, generous house no one seemed to take much notice of trifles.

Ronald went to the dining room. Mrs. Schumacher had come out to change the sprinkler on her lawn, but new curtains again protected him from her curiosity.

Many times Ronald had studied the dining room through his peephole, but to walk in and stand by his old place at the table was a strange experience. In a matrix of familiarity, so much was new. The old dark paneling had been enameled a pale tan, or bisque; the table and chairs were pale wood, of modern light construction, but very charming with the bowl of marigolds on the table.

Three soft steps took him into the front hall. The stairs to the second floor sucked at his gaze, drew his attention up the new red stair runner toward the second floor and the girls' bedrooms. Ronald looked dubiously toward the front door, through which any of five people might unexpectedly return home.

Ronald hesitated. He wanted to explore the living room, even more he wished to visit the second floor. But the front door exhaled sheer menace, as if it only waited until he committed himself before bursting open wide. Ronald drew back and retreated into the kitchen. Here he paused to settle himself. His trepidation was by no means sheer foolishness; it was never wise to ignore a hunch. And there was always the chance that someone might come home when they weren't expected; sooner or later it was sure to happen. If ever he risked the second floor, he must decide upon a place to hide, in case of emergency — such as under a bed. The prospect was not unattractive. If only he dared.

Not today. The front door had given him qualms; he would risk no more adventures. In compensation, he made himself a fine peanut butter and jelly sandwich, and gulped down another cupful of milk. To minimize his depredations, he poured a cupful of water back into the carton, and then he returned to his lair.

Friday passed, then the weekend. On Tuesday Mrs. Wood went off to work and Ronald was again left alone in the house.

At nine o'clock precisely he emerged from his lair, to stand a few minutes in the kitchen listening. No sound. He turned his attention to the refrigerator which yielded a nice dish of applesauce, a good helping of cottage cheese, and a mouthful or two of cold string beans, which he ate for his health's sake. For dessert he raided the cookie jar for three gingersnaps and he allowed himself two swallows of milk. More would be risky, and last Thursday evening the condition of the ice-cream carton had prompted Mrs. Wood to remark, "I thought sure we had more ice cream. It's something we're just not able to keep in this house. A wonder you're not all little chubbies."

With a good breakfast tucked away, Ronald wandered through the dining room and into the front hall. Unlike his mother, the Woods never locked up when they left the house. Burglary was unknown in

Oakmead, and the Woods were trusting by nature. Ronald cleverly protected himself from surprise by locking the door. He was now safe from an unexpected incursion; if anyone tried the door Ronald could hear and be warned. Almost boldly he walked on past the door and into the living room.

He amused himself almost an hour, investigating whatever seemed of interest: the drawer in the desk where Mrs. Wood kept household accounts, canceled checks and letters not yet answered. The photograph album was a fascinating volume. Ronald studied the Wood family in all its stages. Before his eyes the girls grew from babies into toddlers, from tomboys into pretty teenagers. He saw them at picnics and birthday parties, at the beach and in the mountains. He gazed into faces he failed to recognize: relatives, neighbors, family friends; he saw their old house in Los Gatos and their old school, and a number of school pictures.

Ronald finally put away the album and made a last survey of the living room. By sheer chance he happened to glance out the front window and notice a car halting in front of the house: Ben Wood's gray Chevrolet. With heart pounding Ronald loped to the front door, snapped back the latch, and raced through the dining room to his lair. Even as he closed his secret door Ben Wood came into the house. He ran upstairs to his bedroom where he remained only a minute or so, apparently to find some object or document he had forgotten. Then he descended to the ground floor and departed.

Ronald sat hunched on his cot, listening to the footsteps. A close call? Close enough for alarm. The locked door probably would have protected him in any case. Still, the incident went to show that a person couldn't be too careful.

During the afternoon Ronald worked on his nutrition charts. He had lost interest in his projected study of the Wood family; the task now seemed over-complicated and tedious. The fact of the matter was that Ronald had become preoccupied with the upstairs bedrooms. A simple matter to secrete himself under a bed. No one would notice and he could see everything that went on. The idea always brought its own rebuttal. No matter how appealing the project, caution must remain his watchword! So many things might go wrong, and all would mean big trouble. And yet, and yet...Ronald vacillated between conflicting urges. The thought of supple young bodies and the fascinating things which might be accomplished urged him to gallant enterprise. But too much risk, too much risk! What would he do if he were to lose his sanctum? He had no money, no place to go…

On Saturday night Duane Mathews and Ellen went to the movies, thereby incurring Ronald's displeasure. In many ways he found Ellen the most attractive of the girls; he wanted no one fondling her but himself. Ronald watched and listened all evening until, shortly before midnight, Duane brought Ellen home. Ronald heard the car stop, he heard them mount the steps and stand on the porch, and he knew they were kissing.

Ronald grimaced and showed his teeth. He totally disapproved of this sort of thing, and it must be stopped.

On Sunday all three girls went off on a swimming party with Duane and two other boys, and Ronald was left moping and disconsolate all afternoon.

For dinner Mrs. Wood roasted a pair of chickens, the odor of which tantalized Ronald. She also made two beautiful coconut-cream pies. Duane stayed for dinner, and Ronald watched with indignation as he devoured great quantities of everything, which would only mean a near-absence of those leftovers which Ronald had come to count on. But what could he do? Nothing except watch and fight back his rage while Duane wolfed down portion after portion of the food Ronald regarded as his own.

Dinner was over at last and eventually Duane went home. Everyone went to bed and the house became quiet.

Ronald was out of his lair almost at once. As he had feared, the chicken was totally gone. Not a single piece left for him! And nothing else that was any good, except half of one pie. Ronald angrily cut himself a large piece, and it was the most delicious pie he had ever eaten, and he had to have another small helping; after all no one would notice.

But in the morning Mrs. Wood did indeed notice and made a marveling remark to Ellen as to the scope of Duane's appetite. Ellen said in wonder, "He didn't eat any more pie!"

"He must have," said Mrs. Wood. "There was at least half a pie left when I put it away, and your father didn't eat it."

Ellen shook her head in perplexity. "I'm sure it wasn't Duane."

"It doesn't make any difference, of course," said Mrs. Wood. "He's welcome to as much as he can eat. It just seems strange."

Ronald saw Ellen's clear-eyed face take on an unusually doleful expression. Ronald snorted softly. Maybe now she wouldn't think so highly of Duane, who had just earned himself a reputation for gluttony.

Chapter XIII

Within range of Ronald's knowledge, neither Marcia nor Ben Wood seemed ever to discipline their daughters — not only by virtue of their own tolerance, but because the girls gave no provocation for punishment. Barbara occasionally left her room in a mess; Althea tended to question established doctrine on general principle; Ellen was not always punctual, but such delinquencies incurred at worst a pained outcry from Ben or a crisp suggestion from Marcia.

In regard to boys and dating, the senior Woods were reasonable and flexible. The girls knew what was expected of them and the hours they were allowed to keep, and seldom transgressed, and always with explanations and apologies. In general the Woods trusted their daughters' intelligence and mutual reinforcement to keep them out of trouble. Ben gave no lectures in regard to venereal disease; Marcia never stressed the trauma of early marriage or unwanted pregnancy. Between themselves the girls occasionally spoke of sex and its weird variations, and sometimes marveled at the extent to which it permeated the psychological atmosphere.

On very few occasions did the Woods question the judgment of any of their daughters, and that daughter was always Barbara, the most daring and adventurous of the girls. Ellen and Althea despised hippies and the so-called 'counter-culture'; Barbara conceived hippies to be quaint and wild, like gypsies. At Hallowe'en Barbara was invited to a weekend party at Lake Tahoe, but Ben and Marcia for once put their two feet down. Barbara explained that Tamlyn's parents would chaperone; that Lake Tahoe was a place she'd always wanted to visit; that the boys and girls who already had accepted the invitation were in the main respectable. She failed to persuade either Ben or Marcia.

"Too many things could happen, all of them bad," said Ben. "I don't know the Rudnicks; he might be a drunken driver, or a Democrat. Maybe they'd decide to go off and gamble and leave the kids to raise hell on their own. One of the boys might spike the punch with LSD."

"Daddy! You're just being silly."

"Not at all. I'm being mathematical. Look at the odds. Two out of every five drivers on the highway have been drinking and one out of twenty is dead drunk. Three in every ten teenagers smokes marijuana and one out of ten is hooked on LSD or goof-balls or some other stuff. One out of every hundred men is a thug, a rape artist or a con man. At Lake Tahoe the percentage is higher. Five out of every hundred women…"

"Daddy! You're just making this all up!"

"It's close enough to the truth. I'd put the odds at nine out of ten that you'd arrive home in one piece, and that's not good enough."

"Mmfp. I'm just as liable to fall into the bathtub or eat a can of poisoned tuna. I've read that home is the most dangerous place you can be."

"Yes, but at home we've got Band-Aids and stomach pumps and fathers and mothers and sisters. Lake Tahoe is out."

Monday and Friday were the dullest days of the week. Mrs. Wood remained home to curtail Ronald's explorations, and the girls were at school until late afternoon. Junior high let out forty-five minutes earlier than high school; Barbara was usually first to arrive home, though she tended to dally along the way, teasing the boys or gossiping with the girls. Such occasions put Ronald into a mood of nervous irritation. He considered Barbara spoiled, inconsiderate, capricious and utterly adorable. She was rather more aware of her charms than either Althea or Ellen, which made her all the more desirable. Ronald loved her and detested her at the same time — much the emotion he had felt for Laurel Hansen.

On Tuesday Mrs. Wood developed a cold, or an allergic reaction, she wasn't sure which, and stayed home from work. The indisposition persisted during Wednesday, and Ronald was obliged to remain secluded for two extra days. On Thursday Mrs. Wood returned to work, and almost with the closing of the front door Ronald defiantly crawled forth from his lair. He stood listening no more than ten or fifteen seconds, then marched to the refrigerator, where he found only a dish of cold mashed potatoes and a few brussels sprouts. Dared he fry up a pan of bacon and eggs? For three hungry minutes Ronald wavered back and forth. But the bacon was a new unopened package and only four eggs remained on the rack: the missing food would surely be noticed. Ronald ate a peanut butter sandwich and an orange and reluctantly decided against a drink of milk from a nearly empty carton.

His plans for today had already been formed. He went into the living room, looked out into the street, then turned and climbed the stairs.

He barely recognized the upper floor. The hall was painted fresh bright white; on the walls hung a row of gay floral prints, and instead of the old green runner and brown-painted boards, there was now Turkey-red carpeting.

Ronald stood a full two minutes at the head of the stairs; he enjoyed listening to the silence. A car passed along Orchard Street; Ronald froze until the sound diminished and died. If anyone returned unexpectedly he could hide under a bed, but this might be both inconvenient and dangerous.

Ronald moved across the hall. He glanced into the bedroom where his mother had once slept and gave a snort of contempt for the new furnishings. Ellen's room was opposite; to the rear of the house, past the bathroom and the hall closet, were Althea's and Barbara's rooms. Where to start? Perhaps a quick look into all three.

Ellen's room was mostly white, with a lavender ceiling and a pale green rug. This had been his old room! Never in a million years would he have recognized it! He chanced to look in the mirror, and there he saw a face equally different from the old Ronald. The discord between new and old gave him an eerie feeling, as if he were the victim of amnesia or soul-transfer.

On the dresser stood a photograph of Duane Mathews. Ronald scowled down at the bleak bony face and felt a strong temptation to destroy it, or at least blotch out the features with lipstick … Inadvisable.

He turned away to the wardrobe. Ellen's clothes hung in a neat array. Ronald reached forth, stroked the charmed garments which had sheathed that wonderful body! Electric thrills ran up and down his arm. He went back to the dresser and, opening a drawer, inspected her underwear. What intimacy he was now enjoying!

Presently he closed the drawer and stood quietly, breathing slowly and deeply, letting the ambience of the room seep into his skin. Everywhere he could feel Ellen. This mirror had reflected her nudity; here in this chair she had brushed her shining hair; this bed had known the warmth of her body and the scintillating flux of her dreams.

Ronald went to the dressing table. In the top drawer he found a flask of perfume: a soft fruity scent with a hint of violet and just a tang of verbena. He touched a few drops of the perfume to the back of his hand; the bottle slipped and before he could snatch it up, half the liquid had spilled.

Ronald stared in shock. He grabbed a facial tissue and mopped at the tabletop. What to do now? He capped the flask and placed it in the drawer on its side. Ellen would think the perfume had spilled. He took the tissue into the bathroom and flushed it down the toilet. In the hall the scent of perfume still lingered. Oh well, by the time anyone came home, the odor would have dissipated.

Ronald felt uneasy and irritated; the magic was gone from his venture. He returned downstairs and out of sheer disgust stalked into the living room and plumped into one of the easy chairs, where he sat in angry reverie.

He was exposed, he was vulnerable! The front door was not even locked! Guiltily Ronald jumped to his feet and trotted with an elastic bent-kneed gait to safety.

Once more secure in his lair, Ronald lay on the cot. He became aware of the scent of Ellen's perfume, and now it was a nuisance. He went to the washbasin and scrubbed his wrist, and effaced most of the smell. When he regarded the face in the mirror the eerie sense of alienation he had known in Ellen's room was gone; here he was normal ordinary Ronald...

Ronald lay dozing until one o'clock, then cooked himself a lunch of tuna and fried onion pancakes. He decided that his health required one of the Woods' tomatoes, which he fetched from the refrigerator, drinking a gulp of milk from the carton as he did so.

Once again he drowsed until the creak of the front door and light elastic footsteps aroused him. Somewhat lethargically he went to the peephole, but Barbara — he recognized the footsteps — had run directly upstairs.

Ronald stood thinking. Upstairs Barbara; downstairs, himself. The situation had occurred several times previously, but the disadvantages of any sort of action were oppressive. Ronald went back to sit on his cot, and tried to read one of his books... Again footsteps on the front porch. The door opened; Ellen and Althea were home from school. They tossed their books down upon the table in the hall and ran upstairs. Barbara called out a cheery greeting. For a period Ronald heard muffled conversation, which came to a rather abrupt end.

Mrs. Wood returned home and presently Ben Wood. Mrs. Wood served a quick and easy dinner of hamburger sandwiches.

There was an atmosphere at the dinner table. The girls sat silently; evidently they had quarreled. Ben Wood finally asked, "Well, what's happened? Is it a private fight or can we all join in?"

"It's no fight at all," said Ellen. "Just a misunderstanding."

"It's not either a misunderstanding!" Barbara declared. "Ellen thinks I spilled her perfume, and I didn't touch it. I wasn't in her room at all."

Mrs. Wood said, "If you say you didn't do it, you didn't do it. Ellen knows that as well as I do."

"She doesn't believe me."

"Of course I believe you, Bobby!" said Ellen. "It's just all so strange! I could swear someone had been in my room. I don't really care a bit, but the perfume *was* spilled and you can even smell it in the bathroom. I know it wasn't Bobby, but who could it be? It wasn't spilled this morning."

"Odd things happen," said Ben Wood. "There might have been an earthquake, or maybe you closed the drawer too hard. There's a dozen explanations."

Ellen nodded dubiously.

"She still thinks I did it," sulked Barbara. "Deep down she does, and I wasn't even near her room."

"Come now, Babs!" snapped her mother. "Please don't be difficult. Ellen knows you wouldn't lie about such a silly matter, any more than she'd lie to you! It's all so ridiculous!"

"Absolutely, Bobby," said Ellen. "Heavens, I know you better than that! If anything, you're too honest!"

Barbara began to cry, and rising from the table, went into the living room. Ellen went after her and petted her and consoled her.

Ben Wood said, "That's Babs for you. Underneath the foolishness she's the most sensitive of all three."

Althea laughed. "People think I'm sensitive, but I just don't care about things. Ellen cares, but she's so secure! Poor little Babs!"

"The situation is certainly strange," said Ben Wood.

"We might have a poltergeist," said Althea. "They come to houses where young people live. That's well known."

Marcia Wood gave a skeptical snort. "So far I haven't seen objects hurtling through the air, and I don't want to either. I'm not all that interested."

"Oh, I'm interested!" said Althea. "I'd love to experience something strange. Everything happens to other people, never to me."

Ellen and Barbara quietly returned to the dining room and finished their dinner.

Althea said brightly, "We've solved the mystery. It's a poltergeist!"

"No," said Ellen, "I remember now what happened. I closed the drawer very hard this morning and I must have knocked the bottle over."

"Oh! I wanted us to have a poltergeist!"

Ellen smiled and for a flickering instant seemed as mischievous as Barbara at her most outrageous. "Can't we still have him, or her, or it, whatever they are? You know what Duane says."

Mrs. Wood said, "How strange that a boy like Duane, apparently so practical, is superstitious."

"He gets it from his mother," said Ellen. "After Carol was killed, she went to a spiritualist to see if she could talk to Carol's soul, or ghost, or whatever it is."

Mrs. Wood was interested in spite of herself. "What happened?"

"Duane isn't quite sure. His mother thinks she had a message, but

Duane says it might have applied to anyone. He wants her to go back and ask questions that only Carol could answer, and maybe find out where the murderer is now. What was his name?"

"Roderick Wilson, something like that."

"Ronald Wilby," said Barbara.

"And is she going to ask those questions?"

"When she gets around to going. The spiritualist lives in Stockton."

"Don't scoff!" said Ben Wood. "I've heard of spiritualists helping the police many times! There's a Dutchman, I can't think of his name, who solved a half-dozen murders in Holland. These cases are a matter of record."

Ronald hissed between his teeth. Wouldn't people ever stop chewing over that old business? He wanted to hear no more about it. If he hadn't been so foolish and careless, and left the bicycle in the street and his jacket on a bush, no one would know to this day what had happened. Except himself. And Carol's soul, or spirit, or ghost.

Friday: one of the dull days, but Ronald was content to lie quiet in his lair. On Saturday he felt somewhat better, but to his disappointment the girls went off to a football game, returning at five o'clock, only to shower and change and go off again to a party. Ronald sat brooding, his mood rank and bitter as sludge. The girls had flitted off like butterflies, gay and callous, and he was left alone in dreary solitude. He longed to punish them, to even the score. He had felt somewhat the same way about Laurel Hansen until the Carol Mathews business, which in some indirect fashion had wiped clean the slate.

On Sunday Mrs. Wood and the girls drove to San Jose to visit relatives. Mr. Wood stayed home to catch up on paperwork and to watch a football game on television. Another drab day for Ronald. He spent the early part of the afternoon exercising, an activity he had neglected for some time, and the raucous outcry of the sports announcer overwhelmed whatever small sounds he might have made. The day was warm. Ronald discovered himself sweating profusely. He removed his clothes and lay down to rest and drowsed until Mrs. Wood and the girls came home.

They went directly upstairs to bed; Ronald not too enthusiastically busied himself with Atranta.

On Monday Mrs. Wood went shopping. Ronald emerged from his lair to check the refrigerator, but found nothing he cared to eat. In disgust he helped himself to nuts from the fruit bowl and a handful of caramels from a paper bag, then went out into the hall and looked longingly up the stairs. The perfume episode had dwindled in importance; after this he'd naturally take pains to leave no traces. The upstairs tugged at him, but Mrs. Wood might return at any time, and he couldn't risk being caught away from his lair. Even now a car came up Orchard Street, and Ronald hastened back to safety.

The afternoon passed. Ronald waited fretfully for the girls to come home, but Mrs. Wood met Barbara at school and took her to the dentist. Ellen and Althea stayed late to play tennis, so that all arrived home together about six o'clock.

On Tuesday Mrs. Wood went to work. As soon as the front door closed, Ronald crawled out through his own door. He stood in the pantry to listen; it was always wise to be cautious.

No sound save a fly buzzing at the kitchen window. Ronald crossed to the refrigerator where he discovered a package of sliced salami, a bowl of tuna salad, green onions: sufficient material for two excellent sandwiches, which he washed down with a generous helping of milk. By and large, a good breakfast.

Now what? The day lay ahead of him. Ronald went boldly into the living room and peered up and down Orchard Street. The coast was clear. He climbed the stairs to the second floor. Who should it be today: Althea or Barbara? He decided upon Althea.

The room was quite different from Ellen's. On the walls hung Art Nouveau posters, and the shelves supported books with titles unfamiliar to Ronald, among them several volumes of fantasy and others of science fiction. Of the three girls, only Althea's perceptivity even remotely matched his own. She'd be enthralled to know that here, in this very same house, the Atranta sagas had been formulated. Ronald toyed with the idea of writing Althea a letter. There'd be difficulty mailing such a letter, unless he slipped out in the dead of night to the mailbox at the corner. He'd have to commandeer an envelope and a stamp from the desk in the living room…Well, perhaps he wouldn't bother.

He investigated the drawers of her desk and this time took extra care not to handle anything which might spill or leak…What was this? Ronald brought forth a book bound in green simulated leather, with a locked flap across the edge. On the front, in gold leaf, was stamped the word *Diary*.

Ronald turned the book this way and that. He tugged gently at the strap, but the lock held the book shut.

Ronald put down the book and searched for the key; Althea would certainly not carry it on her person. He inspected the underside of all the drawers, ran his finger along the picture molding, checked the contents of the jewelry box, investigated the structural members of bed and chairs. No key. Baffled, Ronald picked up the diary, which breathed a soundless music whose purport he could not even guess. Where was the dratted key? He searched the bedside table, the Mexican pottery piggy bank, the pencil cup on the windowsill. No key. Ronald scrutinized the book. He worked the strap back and forth, trying to disengage the clasp. He bent a paper clip, fitted it into the lock, twisted. Something seemed to move. Ronald twisted more vigorously and the end of the paper clip broke off in the lock. Ronald muttered a curse. The broken end could not be dislodged. Inside the keyhole he could see the shine of metal, but no effort would dislodge it.

Well then, what to do? He knew himself to be resourceful and keen; now was the time to demonstrate his craft. Perhaps he could take the lock apart and repair it. Only rivets secured the lock to the simulated leather…Impractical; he had no tools. Perhaps he should simply remove the diary and hide it. Althea after all was an absentminded girl: so everyone in the family, including Althea, pretended to believe. She might not notice its loss for months.

The idea was unsound. A diary, by definition, was used daily. By squinting into the pages Ronald could see that Althea wrote regularly in the book.

A real problem. If he had another similar diary he might attempt to transfer the covers. Then, of course, Althea's key wouldn't fit—

unless one key fit all such diaries. In any event, he had access to no such duplicate diary.

In a dispirited mood Ronald tried to disengage the piece of broken wire with a nail file, but only succeeded in scratching the nickel-plating on the housing, and bending the lip of the keyhole. Now sweating, Ronald tried to repair the damage. Althea probably wouldn't notice; none of the girls were particularly observant or critical... But how he wished he could remove that dratted bit of broken wire! Perhaps if he pried up the cover plate — but he could never replace it. He took the paper clip and furiously worried the bit of broken wire: prodding, poking, prying — all to no effect.

Ronald quietly put the diary where he had found it. He was disgusted with the whole thing. Althea might be puzzled, but she wasn't a girl to fret over trifles; she might not even notice. Probably when she put the key in the lock the wire would come loose. Ronald smoothed the bed where he had sat on it, closed all the drawers, and returned gloomily downstairs.

The time was now about noon. Ronald helped himself to a nice chunk of hamburger, two slices of bread and butter, half an onion and a tomato. Sliding into the lair, he cooked the meat in his pan and contrived a very tasty sandwich indeed. In fact, he could easily consume another of the same. Alas, too risky. He contented himself with a good helping of ice cream topped with strawberry jam and a squirt of synthetic cream.

The afternoon lay before him. He went into the living room and sat where he could watch the street. Today Barbara might well be home early. If he went upstairs and hid in her bedroom closet he could watch her changing clothes. When she went to hang up her dress, there he'd be... It wouldn't be so bad if he could spend a whole day or even half a day with her. He'd pretend to be an intruder, and she'd never recognize him as Ronald Wilby. Hmm. The idea was not all that impractical. He could tie her to the bed, go downstairs, slam the front door, then hasten back to his lair. What a hullabaloo there'd be! He'd enjoy every minute of it. Then in a month or so, he'd do the same thing again! Ellen and Althea coming home so soon made the project impossible. Too bad, because otherwise the exploit would be perfectly safe and Barbara, sexy little scamp that she was, wouldn't be all that reluctant. And if she were, so what?

Two o'clock. He'd better be getting back in his lair. Perhaps some day Barbara would be home by herself. Or Althea. Or Ellen.

He lay on his cot, deep in reflection. Since he'd started exploring upstairs he'd neglected everything — charts, exercise, Atranta. He especially wanted to get back to Atranta, where an enormous amount of work remained to be done.

Shortly before four Barbara arrived home, and ran directly upstairs to change from her school clothes. Almost at once the telephone rang and Barbara came flying back downstairs wearing only brassiere and underpants. Ronald, with his eye to the peephole, ecstatically sucked in his breath; never had he seen so enchanting a sight — save one time before. He was hard put to control himself; he made soft moaning sounds under his breath and moved his head back and forth to obtain a better view. If only he had time and opportunity! He'd take his chances with the consequences!

Barbara chatted on the phone for twenty minutes. First she sat on the arm of the sofa, then slumped backwards down upon the cushion, with her knees hooked over the arm. She raised one leg, pointed her toes toward the ceiling. Ronald gasped and sighed. She swung around and sat with one leg curled under herself, then sprawled back with both legs stretched out to the floor, and Ronald bit his lips to muffle a hoarse whisper...Had she heard him! She looked up suddenly with an odd expression, but it was only for a passing car. She rose to her feet and with her back to Ronald, still holding the telephone to her ear, looked out into the street. The conversation came to an end; Barbara hung up the receiver and trotted back upstairs. Ronald stood clenching and unclenching his fists. He sat down on his couch, feeling faint.

The front door opened to admit Ellen and Althea.

"Hello!" cried Ellen. "Who's home? Anybody?"

From upstairs came Barbara's voice, "Just me. But I'm enough."

Ellen went into the kitchen. "I'm starving. I wonder if any cookies are left... A few." She opened the refrigerator, and there was a moment of silence. Then Ronald heard her call in a hushed voice, "Althea, would you look at this!"

Althea came into the kitchen. "Isn't that awful! We ought to make a complaint!"

"Uk," said Ellen. "Let's just throw it out."

"Better not waste it," said Althea. "If I cut it off about here, it'll be OK. After all the hair just caught on the top of the carton."

"I guess we can't sue anyone. Things like that are so disgusting."

"Every loaf of bread is one-half of one percent rat dirt, or some such amount. We shouldn't be all that finicky, because it's useless to start with."

"Think of that!" said Ellen. "For ten loaves of bread we pay almost four dollars. One-half of one percent — that's two cents. Every time we buy ten loaves of bread, we get two cents worth of rat dirt."

"That's no bargain."

The girls went back into the dining room.

"I think I'll do my French right now," said Althea, "and have it all finished before dinner."

"I promised Mom I'd water the lawn. We've got to keep up with the Schumachers. I'm going to change clothes first."

The girls went upstairs where their voices became an unintelligible babble.

Then there was silence. After a few minutes Ellen came downstairs and went out to water the lawn.

Marcia Wood arrived home and then Ben Wood. Mrs. Wood started to prepare dinner. Ben Wood took a glass of sherry into the living room and read the newspaper.

At six-thirty Mrs. Wood served dinner. The table was very quiet; and the usual chatter was conspicuous by its absence. Ben Wood spoke in a fretful voice, "What's the trouble tonight? Why all the long faces?"

"No trouble whatever," said Althea. "We're all busy eating."

"I love tacos," said Ellen. "Tonight I want at least a dozen."

"Oh come now," said Ben Wood. "I can tell something is wrong. Maybe I shouldn't ask?"

"I'll tell you what's wrong," declared Barbara in a voice filled with emotion. "Allie thinks I tried to get into her diary."

"I didn't say anything of the sort," Althea replied in a tight voice. "I said somebody had been trying to open my diary, and that's all I said."

"But you meant me, because you said it was all right last night and now the lock's broken, and I was home before you were, so you were accusing me, and I didn't do it, and I'm sick of being blamed for everything. I'll run away and join the hippies unless people stop acting like I'm a sneak—"

"*As if* I'm a sneak," said Ellen.

"—because I'm not. I'm not interested in your diary, and even if I were I wouldn't touch it, and I didn't touch Ellen's perfume either. I don't care what you think, but I'm just not going to sit here and have everybody calling me a sneak!"

"Come now, come now!" declared Ben Wood. "Less tantrum and more fact!"

"I really don't want to talk about it," said Althea with dignity. "I'm sorry I ever mentioned it."

"You see?" cried Barbara. "She thinks I looked in her diary!"

"No I don't. Nobody looked in the diary. Somebody *tried* to look in it!"

Ellen spoke in a hushed, only half-humorous, voice, "Maybe we do have a poltergeist!"

Mrs. Wood said, "It couldn't be neighborhood children. There aren't any on the block. Mrs. Schumacher would certainly notice if anyone walked into our house."

"Unless it's Mrs. Schumacher herself," suggested Ben Wood. "Old women often get a bit strange."

"With her sore hip and Mr. Schumacher sick?" demanded Marcia Wood. "It's just not reasonable."

"Oh well," said Ellen, then lapsed into silence, and dinner proceeded in an atmosphere of strain.

Ronald meanwhile sat on his cot, head cradled in his hands, elbows on knees. Althea had noticed after all, and once again Barbara had been blamed…As good a solution to the problem as any. Barbara, proud spoiled Babs, flouncing around, always performing and swinging her rump as if she were some big-time sexpot, it was good to see her taken down a peg. It was no big thing, anyway. There'd be puzzlement for a day or two, then everybody would forget the matter…Barbara! He couldn't get her out of his mind. Babs, in her skimpy underpants!

Enough to turn a strong man's bones to jelly, and that's the way he felt right now: perturbed, hectic, limp, tired.

Wednesday morning and the atmosphere at breakfast was cool. Ellen was pensive; Althea, remote; Barbara, silent and sulky. Marcia and Ben Wood tried to enliven the occasion; they spoke of Ben's imminent promotion to Classification 15-E, qualifying him for division management; they discussed the possibility of a weekend trip into the mountains, but the conversation was stiff and uneasy, and the girls contributed nothing.

The night before, in the privacy of their bedroom, Ben and Marcia had talked over the affair, and had decided that maybe Barbara, notoriously emotional and famous for pranks and tricks, had attempted some sort of strange adolescent joke which had misfired and now couldn't bring herself to admit it. Both agreed that Barbara, no matter what, was emphatically not sly; never would she try to peek into Althea's diary; if she wanted to know something, she'd merely ask Althea, who no doubt would tell her as a matter of course. The whole affair was grotesque, completely out of character.

In their own ways, Ellen and Althea had both arrived at the same conclusion. Still, if not Barbara, who? Ellen thought it might be Joel Watkins, a boy currently pursuing Althea with rather unwelcome attentions. Joel was known to be both brash and irresponsible, but would he dare enter their house and try to read Althea's diary? Unlikely. Also, Joel had been at school all day Tuesday and couldn't possibly have visited the Wood house.

So then: who?

Her father and mother? Absurd. But the whole affair was absurd — and not a little frightening! The person who suffered most was Bobby, who carried on existence in a most uncharacteristic silence. She was the most obvious suspect, and knew it, and resented the situation intensely.

Thursday morning, on the way to school, Ellen had a chance to say a few words to Barbara, "I know you're brooding about that silly diary, but don't. Everybody knows you wouldn't do a thing like that."

"Everybody doesn't know it," said Barbara. "Whenever the subject comes up, nobody looks at me. I'd give anything to know what happened."

On Thursday morning Ronald felt taut and edgy, for a reason which hovered just past the brink of his consciousness, but conveniently at hand in case he really wanted to know. He even felt a bit queasy, like an athlete before competition. Imminence hung in the air.

When Mrs. Wood left for work, he did not immediately sally forth into the kitchen, but remained sitting on the edge of his cot, staring down at the floor. With a somewhat pedantic assiduity he took note of his symptoms: a twitching of the skin, delicacy at the front of the stomach, a slight sense of dimensional displacement, or vertigo: sensations odd but not unpleasant.

Ronald heaved a mournful sigh and tried to arrange his thoughts. Nothing came. Those thoughts he sought to grapple fled like thieves; others skulked off in the region of the subconscious. All right then, said Ronald, if that's the way it was, let the subconscious do all the thinking and let the acting take care of itself.

Ronald pursed out his lips at this idea. Very sound. History crawled thick with ditherers. Ronald heaved another sigh, exhaling all his doubts and qualms. It was really so easy. What must be, must be. How blissful was this thought. Destiny flowed like a mighty river. He, Ronald, was another such inexorable surge. If he and destiny tried to flow in opposite directions, the result was turmoil, just a lot of thrashing around. Either destiny must join his direction, or he must swerve to join with destiny. It saved a lot of time and discussion if he, Ronald, were the flexible one, and this was how things were. He rode with destiny, buoyant and free, ignoring trivial distractions, without regard for past or future. A single time existed; that time was now. There was nothing else; there never would be anything else. Time and destiny and Ronald Arden Wilby, three elemental vectors converging to a focus like the Mercedes-Benz insignia. The three were one; the one was three, and this was the way it must be.

Ronald rose to his feet, tingling with power. He opened his secret door, crawled out into the kitchen, and gnawed on a piece of cold chicken. Then he went into the living room and sat where he could watch the street. The front door was locked and the key was hidden under the steps. Today Ben Wood was having new keys to the front door cut; hereafter the house would always be locked.

The prospect meant nothing to Ronald. His mother had always locked up… His mother! He had not thought of her recently. Dear old Mother! The denizen of a far age, like Queen Victoria.

The hours went by slowly. Ronald was not impatient. He felt calm yet highly sentient, as if he had been taking a time-dilating drug. Images flickered through his mind: Barbara in her flimsy little briefs. How she loved to pose and twist and thrust out her breasts! To own such beauty and flaunt it the way she did was inexcusable provocation. So be it, so be it. A girl like that simply demanded to be taken care of. So be it.

The mantle clock chimed twelve noon. Ronald strolled into the kitchen, assembled and consumed a peanut butter, mayonnaise and banana sandwich. He felt quite cool; he was pleased to notice that his movements were exact and deliberate. The result, possibly, of entering what might be called 'phase three'. For he was now truly independent, self-sufficient, alone: himself against the world! So be it! He feared nothing; his lair was an impenetrable bastion, so long as he made no noise… In a way, he felt as if he were really someone new, or, more accurately, his basic self: a person unhampered, unshackled, indomitable! Once a person became one with — 'Destiny' wasn't quite the right word. Fate? Cosmos? Oh well, no great matter. Whenever a person merged with this massive force — whatever it was — anything became possible, whatever the mind could imagine! Within reason of course. He couldn't very well fly through the air, or run a mile in thirty seconds, but any ordinary feat was possible.

Craft and foresight of course were the indispensable adjuncts to boldness. Ronald carefully replaced the bread in the bread box, took the margarine and the jar of peanut butter to the refrigerator, rinsed and dried the knife, and put it in the drawer.

The time was one o'clock. Ronald returned to his lair and lay on the cot, tingling to his new vitality… The charts on the wall distracted him. They looked stale and tiresome; they belonged to a different time of his life. He roused himself from the cot and took them down. Better, much better. Exercise? Not just now, he wasn't in the mood. He wanted only to lie on the cot and expand into the new sensations he had discovered.

Three o'clock. His mouth felt somewhat furry; he gave his teeth a good scrubbing. Niceties of this sort were the hallmarks of a gentleman, so his mother had insisted. He frowned down at his fingernails. They probably could use some attention. His mother had also laid much stress upon well-trimmed and clean fingernails. Just now he was not disposed to dwell upon his mother and her precepts. A wonderful woman, of course, if just a bit old-fashioned and conventional. Ronald stretched his arms, scratched his jowls. Should he shave? He allowed the matter to slide from his mind, but he brushed at his hair, which was somewhat untidy. Still, long hair was currently stylish, so it made no great difference.

The time was twenty minutes after three. Ronald crawled out into the kitchen, padded into the living room and stood by the window. The blood sang in his veins; never had he felt so alive, so sure and steady… Of course it was quite possible that Barbara would stay late at school, in which case — a tiresome thought. Anyway there she came now, in a short gray-blue skirt and a dark red pullover. He retreated up the stairs to the landing and waited in the shadows.

The doorknob turned without effect. Barbara had forgotten that the door was locked. She went back for the key.

The door opened. Barbara came into the house, rather less jauntily than usual. She wandered into the dining room, dropped her books on the table, then turned her head, as if an odd odor or unexpected sound had impinged on her consciousness. After a moment she went on into the kitchen and stopped by the refrigerator for an apple and a glass of milk. She decided to sit downstairs for a while, until Ellen and Althea came home. After those strange things which had been happening upstairs, the old house didn't seem as secure as it had during the summer.

She closed the refrigerator door, turned back toward the dining room, and there stood Ronald, looming in the doorway.

"Hello," said Ronald.

She stared at him.

Ronald smiled a modest kind smile. "You don't know me. But I know you."

CHAPTER XIV

BARBARA THOUGHT, I mustn't get nervous, I mustn't show I'm scared. That only excites people like this. Act as casual as possible. She asked, without hardly a quaver in her voice, "Well then — who are you?"

Ronald chuckled. "My name could be anything. Norbert, the Duke of Kastifax, for instance."

"That's an odd name. What are you doing in our house? You'd better leave, and quick, unless you want my father to catch you."

"He won't be home for two hours. Drink your milk."

"Drink my milk?" Barbara looked in puzzlement down at the glass. Perhaps she could throw it at him and run out the back door. He came two steps closer. Barbara shrank back against the sink. To keep him away she raised the glass and forced two or three gulps down her throat. Ronald, smiling pleasantly, reached for the glass. Barbara moved it indignantly back beyond his reach. "I'm not finished!" Anything to gain time, even a few minutes. She raised the glass again and sipped, but Ronald was not about to be flimflammed by a ruse so transparent. He took the glass, poured what was left down the sink, rinsed it and put it back on the shelf. "Come along," he said.

Barbara shook her head. "I've got homework to do." Her voice still was fairly firm. "Why don't you have some ice cream? Then you can help me with my math."

"This way," said Ronald.

"I don't want to," said Barbara, and now the quaver was evident. She suddenly tried to run into the dining room, but Ronald caught her arm and swung her smartly back. The contact between their bodies worked an abrupt change upon Ronald. His smile vanished; she felt

— 109 —

him quivering and straining, and now she could no longer control herself. She screamed. Ronald instantly clapped his hand over her mouth. For a moment they stood tense and poised, motionless except for the glances Ronald darted out the window...He exhaled, relaxed. There was no one to hear. He turned his attention back to Barbara.

"Listen!" said Ronald in a husky voice. "Listen carefully! Because you'll be sorry if you don't. Do you hear?" He gave her a shake. "Do you hear?"

Barbara nodded, her throat too full for words.

Ronald took his hand from her mouth. "You do exactly what I tell you! Exactly! Otherwise — well, I won't say. Do you understand?"

"Yes," mumbled Barbara.

"Come along then. Into the pantry."

"No, no," wailed Barbara. The idea was absurd. "Why into the pantry?"

"Just do what you're told. Don't ask questions. Get down on your hands and knees."

"Oh, no, no! Please don't!"

Ronald cuffed the side of her face; Barbara gasped in terror. At last she understood the dimensions of her predicament. Here was a situation against which her cleverness and charm were useless. Yes, yes; she'd do anything, to keep herself from — the word wouldn't surface into her mind. She dropped to her hands and knees and crawled into the pantry, to freeze in sheer amazement to see the secret doorway, with the light shining forth from the lair.

"Go on in," said the dark shape behind her. She winced at the tremble of excitement in his voice. She slid through the door into the lair.

"Sit down on the cot," said Ronald. He gave her paper and a ballpoint pen, and put a book on her knees. "Write exactly what I tell you."

He dictated and Barbara, blinking through tears, wrote.

Ronald read the finished product. "That's good enough. Now sit here, and don't move until I get back." He crouched to leave by the secret door, then turned to look back at Barbara. "I don't want to scare you, but I want to make sure you understand. Do exactly as I tell you, or we'll have trouble."

Barbara nodded mournfully, the tears now streaming down her face.

Ronald hesitated, then rose once more to his feet. "I better not take any chances," he muttered. "You just might try something crazy. Lie down."

"What are you going to do?" cried Barbara, her voice quavering in and out of hysteria.

Ronald pushed her down on the cot; Barbara lost control of herself. She fought and kicked. Ronald cuffed her twice, on each side of the face, the way tough guys did it in the movies. Barbara gasped and drew in her breath to scream. Ronald ominously drew back his hand; Barbara held her breath in terror. For ten seconds they stared into each other's faces, then Ronald slowly lowered his hand. Barbara lay quiet, as if mesmerized.

Ronald lashed her ankles to the bottom of the cot, tied her wrists together and gagged her with a rag. "Maybe this is unnecessary," he said in a gruff voice, "but I can't take chances on anything."

He dropped to his hands and knees and slid through the secret door with the note. Barbara strained at the cords, but they held securely. She looked desperately around the lair. How weird and colorful, with every square inch covered with drawings, maps, portraits...Ronald returned. He closed and fastened the secret door. Barbara did not dare to look at him. She knew who he was: Ronald Wilby, the murderer, and she knew who had spilled Ellen's perfume, and who had broken Althea's diary.

He dropped to his knees beside her and took the gag from her mouth. Barbara lay quiet, breathing shallowly. For ten or fifteen seconds Ronald searched her face. Then in a soft voice he said, "If you make a sound or try to attract attention — do you know what I'll do?"

She whispered, "You'll kill me."

Ronald nodded gravely and began to untie her. "I'd have to. I don't want to. I'd just have to. When anybody is in the house, you lie on the cot and be quiet! Not a sound. Because you'd never make another...I don't want to scare you, but you've got to know what the situation is."

"Whether you want to scare me or not," said Barbara, "I'm scared! I don't want to be in here! What are you going to do with me?"

Ronald, once more urbane, grinned at her. "Don't you know?"

"No!"

"Come now," said Ronald in a playful voice. "Don't be difficult." He considered a minute. "This was my old secret lair, from when I was a little boy. I came back here just a few days ago, to see what had happened to the house. In a few days I'm going away again, and then you can do whatever you please — come with me, if you want to. Maybe we'll like each other by then."

Barbara bit her lower lip, to hold back a shriek of hysterical laughter.

"We can only talk for a few minutes," said Ronald, "because your sisters will be home, and then we'll have to be quiet. Take off your clothes."

This was the time she had been dreading. Still, measured against the other circumstances, it wasn't all that much worse... A nightmare! Oh please, Barbara, wake up, wake up! The faces in the portraits; the grotesque castles; the dark red, purple, black and green rooms: unreal, unreal, unreal!

"Take off your clothes!" said Ronald gently. "You're so beautiful!... I'll help you."

Barbara's fingers were numb. Clumsily, as slowly as possible, she undressed. She could not bring herself to remove her underthings; Ronald pulled them off, hissing through his teeth while she kept her eyes squeezed shut.

Ronald slipped out of his own soiled garments. He glanced at the clock. Ten minutes, maybe fifteen, before anyone came home. He loomed upon her, stroked her body, kissed her. Barbara gasped. "Remember!" Ronald warned her, "not a sound!"

Ellen and Althea came home. "Hello!" called Ellen. "Who's here? Anyone?"

"Barbara!" Althea yelled, and then to Ellen, "She's not home yet."

"She's probably at the tennis court, the little wretch. Barbara?"

No reply. They went into the dining room and there on the table lay a sheet of paper. Ellen picked it up and read. "Oh, no!"

"What is it?"

Ellen showed her the note. Althea read, and the two girls looked at each other in consternation.

"Why, it's fantastic!" cried Althea. "Of course we trusted her! Poor little Babs!"

"We'd better telephone Daddy."

They ran into the living room. With quick fingers Ellen twisted the telephone dial. "Mr. Wood, please…Daddy? This is Ellen. We just got home, Althea and I. Barbara isn't here. She left a note. Listen, this is what she says,

> *Dear Everybody:*
> *Nobody trusts me and I can't stand it anymore. I've gone*
> *off to join the hippies. I'll be back after a while. Don't worry*
> *about me, I'll be all right.*
> *Barbara.*

From the telephone came only the hum of the wire. Ellen cried out, "Daddy? Did you hear?"

Ben Wood spoke in a harsh voice, "Is this some kind of a joke?"

"She's not home," declared Ellen. "You know that she's been acting strangely. I hope it's a joke."

"I'm coming right home. Have you called your mother?"

"Not yet."

"Call her, then notify the police. I'll be right there."

Five minutes later Ben Wood raced up the steps and into the house. Ellen and Althea had further information for him. "She didn't take any of her clothes!" "And she left all the money in her piggy bank!" "She didn't take anything!"

Marcia Wood came running into the house, and for a few moments there was confusion with everyone talking at once. Then Ben Wood telephoned the police department once more and was notified that a bulletin had been passed on to the Highway Patrol. Marcia Wood decided to visit the bus station. She took a photograph of Barbara to show the ticket-sellers and departed. Ellen and Althea telephoned Barbara's friends and asked if they knew anything of her whereabouts. Ben Wood went out in his car and drove to all the likely hitchhiking places at the edge of town and questioned anyone who might have seen Barbara.

At eight o'clock Ben and Marcia had returned home, without news of any kind. Ellen warmed some canned tomato soup, made toast, and insisted that her mother and father eat.

The makeshift dinner was a grim occasion. Everyone was edgy and spoke in strained high-pitched voices. What demon of perversity had prompted gay little Barbara to such a desperate act? The situation was incredible, and no one could really believe it had happened. Still, the evidence was stark and simple: Barbara was gone.

"She's a temperamental person," said Ellen. "But she's not crazy. I just can't believe she'd do a thing like this. She doesn't like hippies any more than we do."

Marcia Wood looked up in consternation. "You think she didn't go off of her own free will?"

"It's a possibility."

Ben Wood said dubiously, "There wasn't any sign of a struggle."

"There was an apple on the kitchen floor," said Althea. "I picked it up. It had teeth-marks in it."

Ben Wood went into the living room and once more called the police. He returned to the dining table muttering curses under his breath. "They take the matter so damn casually. I can't believe they're doing anything!"

Marcia Wood smiled bitterly. "They're used to runaways. It happens every day or so, and no doubt every family tells them the same thing."

"But our family is different!" cried Ellen. "If they don't believe it, I'll go down and tell them!"

"Don't bother," growled Ben Wood. "It wouldn't do any good."

"I've got a better idea," said Althea. "If she went off by herself, she probably headed for Berkeley. I'd like to go there too and walk up and down Telegraph Avenue. I bet I'd find her sooner or later!"

Her mother vetoed the idea.

"We've got to do something!" Althea cried. "We can't just sit here!"

"If I could think of something to do," said Ben Wood, "I'd do it."

The doorbell rang; Ellen ran into the hall and opened the door. She returned with Duane, to whom she had already communicated the news. "I don't know if there's anything I can do," said Duane, "but if there is, just tell me."

"Thanks, Duane," said Marcia. "We know that already."

"We're just sitting here gnawing our nails," said Althea. "If only we had some sort of clue, or knew somebody she might have gone with, or gone to — there's just nothing."

"What about Los Gatos? Would she want to go back there?"

"I can't imagine why," said Ben Wood. "Nothing is sensible to begin with. Los Gatos is as good a guess as any."

"I can't understand it," said Duane. "Babs sometimes acted foolish, but she was really a sensible kid. She wouldn't run away from home like this!"

Ben Wood leaned wearily back in his chair. "I've heard of a wildness, or a psychosis, that comes over adolescents and makes them do all manner of strange things. Maybe this is what happened to Babs."

Duane shook his head. "She isn't any crazier than I am — and I'm not crazy. There's something very strange going on."

"I wish I knew what." Ben Wood rose to his feet and stood indecisively. "We're all worn out. Probably we should go to bed and try to get some rest."

"I couldn't sleep," Althea declared. "I'd just be thinking about Babs…We should be out looking for her! Daddy, Mom, why don't we drive into Berkeley? There's a chance in a million we might find her!"

Ben Wood shook his head gloomily. "The chances of getting killed on the freeway are better than that."

The talk went on. Inside the lair Ronald and Barbara listened, the first indifferently, the second in anguish. Ronald had taken steps to forestall even an involuntary outcry. He had fixed a gag to her mouth, and also had looped a cord around her neck with a single overhand knot under her chin. One end of the cord he tied to a stud in the wall beside the cot, the other he held in his hand. If Barbara so much as squeaked, he could jerk the noose tight, to cut off her breath. To prevent any noisy thrashing about he had lashed her ankles to the cot.

He sat with his ear to the wall. Inasmuch as the light was on, he had covered over the peephole. Why didn't they all go to bed? And Duane Mathews: he had no business around here. His offers of help were just so much malarky; Duane only wanted a chance to get next to Ellen!

The Woods finally trooped upstairs to bed. Ellen and Duane stood talking on the front porch for a few minutes, then she too went up to her room.

Ronald removed the gag from Barbara's mouth and untied her ankles. She watched with dull apprehension. Ronald sat on the cot beside her. He said, "You can't imagine how long I've wanted to do this."

Barbara spoke in a strained whisper, "I thought you said you'd just come back."

Ronald gave a patient little laugh. "I come and go. But this is my home. In fact, it's my world, my very own! What you see on the walls I've created!"

Barbara gazed incuriously at the pictures. "What does it mean?"

"It's the magic land of Atranta!" said Ronald in a rich, if muted, voice. "See the map? It shows the six duchies and Zulamber the City of Blue-green Pearls. These are portraits of the dukes, and this is Norbert, from Vordling, who defeated Duke Urken. I know them as well as I know myself. They're as real to me as you are. Would you like to hear the history of Atranta?"

Barbara closed her eyes. The more energy expended in talk, the less remained for lust. Maybe he'd get excited, and somebody would hear him. Maybe he'd relax and forget to tie the noose around her neck. "Yes," she said. "Tell me about it."

"After a while," said Ronald craftily. "Right now I'm more interested in you. I just love to look at you. You've got the most beautiful body I've ever seen. I never thought anything could be so wonderful."

Barbara licked her lips. He was crazy, or so she supposed. Or maybe he wasn't. Certainly she didn't dare antagonize him. The lovemaking she could tolerate, but if she ever got free — when she got free — she'd wash and wash and wash; she'd never get enough of it: baths, showers, douches, gargling. Even then she knew she'd never feel quite clean again. Somehow she'd have to use her wits. But not now: Ronald was intent on lovemaking.

Ronald lay beside her, lethargic and lax. She hated the feel of his body; the skin felt sticky and greasy, and he exuded an odd musky odor like wax crayons or cows mixed with codfish and the pine boxes in which codfish came packed, and more than a taint of the stable or the outhouse. She wondered how often Ronald bathed. Was he dozing? She dared make no move to ease her own cramped position lest he awake and become amorous again, although now it didn't make all that much difference; it was even a break in the monotony. She wondered what Ronald really intended to do with her. He couldn't keep her in the lair forever; there wouldn't be enough food. Certainly he wouldn't just let her go free. Somehow, of course, she'd escape or be rescued — impossible to imagine anything else with her father and mother so close! Still, if ever in her life she needed strength and resource, the time was now!

So long as she pleased him and obeyed his orders, she could expect to escape serious harm…How could she signal her parents without arousing Ronald's suspicions?…There might be a way.

"Ronald," she said softly.

He was instantly awake, or perhaps he had never been asleep. "Yeah?"

"How long are we going to stay in here?"

Ronald chuckled. "Don't you like it?"

"It's a little cramped."

"It doesn't seem cramped to me. Look at those pictures and the map: right away you're in Atranta. I'm Norbert and you're Fansetta. In the Great History she sent out a troop of black-and-yellow trolls, and they trapped him with a song that doesn't have any end. When you start singing it you can't find the place to stop. They carried him along this path here —" Ronald reached over to touch the map "— around the Three Crags to Glimmis. That's a castle here on Misty Moor. When he wouldn't marry her she chained him to an old statue of black copper and lashed him with a whip woven of scorpion tails."

"I don't want to be Fansetta then, because I wouldn't do a thing like that. Isn't there someone nicer I could be?"

Ronald deliberated. "Mersilde is a cloud-witch. She's cruel but very beautiful. Then there's Darrue, a girl half-fairy and half-ghowan…"

"What's a 'ghowan'?"

"It's a kind of a cave-elf, very pale and mysteriously beautiful. A ghowan has hair like white silk, his eyes are like glass balls with little glinting stars in them. Darrue loves Norbert, but she doesn't dare show herself to him, because when a ghowan kisses a mortal, it takes a fever and dies, and Darrue doesn't know whether she's mostly fairy or mostly ghowan."

"I'd just as soon be someone beautiful who doesn't need to worry so much."

"Hmm. I don't know about that." Ronald was now fully awake, and aware of the girl's body beside him. He began to fondle her, and Barbara lay submissive.

He paused in his exertions to look down at her. He said in a husky voice, "I like this. Do you?"

Barbara groped for words, and came up with one of her insane frivolities. "Well — it's free." She realized that this wasn't quite positive enough. Above all, she must soothe Ronald's vanity and keep his antagonism in check. "And — well, exciting."

"You can't imagine how much I've wanted to do this," Ronald panted, "with you... And now..."

Barbara closed her eyes and turned her head, to keep Ronald's hair out of her face, and presently Ronald spent himself.

A moment or so later he asked, "Like it?"

Unwilling to trust her voice, Barbara nodded.

"What's it like?" asked Ronald.

"I don't know," said Barbara, desperately damming back hysteria, which could only affect Ronald adversely. "It's just — exciting."

"What do you think of me now?"

Ronald tried to sound casual and worldly. Before Barbara could frame a reply, he said, "I realize that we met in a kind of unusual way, and I had to act as I did to get you in here — but now that we've made love together — well, you must have some sort of feelings about me."

"I wish I had met you in the usual way," said Barbara cautiously.

"But then we'd never have gotten this far, lying together like this, without our clothes on."

Barbara wondered as to the exact level of Ronald's credulity. "You never can tell. In fact it would be nice if we could go somewhere where there's more room, up into the mountains, maybe where we could camp, under the trees."

Ronald raised up on an elbow. She could feel his instant suspicion. "Lovely. But we don't have any money. At least I don't. Do you?"

"Just what's in my bank — about twelve dollars."

"That wouldn't take us very far."

Barbara became silent. The outlook was grim. She stirred. Ronald was instantly alert. "What are you doing?"

"I want to use the toilet."

"OK. But don't flush it. We've got to wait until somebody upstairs uses the bathroom."

"Oh."

"And make sure you're quiet…I won't look."

Barbara found Ronald's delicacy intensely droll. But she dared not laugh. She might not be able to stop.

The night passed. Ronald insisted that Barbara sleep on the inside of the cot, against the wall, where she felt stifled and cramped. Somehow she slept, fitfully and without comfort.

For breakfast Ronald served boiled eggs and toast with margarine and jam. Barbara politely forebore to discuss the source of Ronald's supplies.

Her family came downstairs and Ronald again made her lie on the cot, with the noose around her neck. "I don't like to do this," Ronald whispered, "but there's no other way. You might just take a crazy notion to yell."

Oh, for the chance! If he'd be careless a single instant — oh, how she'd yell, so her father could hear, and she'd do her best to fight off Ronald…Except that her father might not be able to find his way into the lair in time to save her.

Ronald watched the Woods eat breakfast. Barbara lay tense and sweating, thinking of the days and weeks and months she had lived careless and free with Ronald's avid gaze on her. Althea had often complained of the atmosphere which pervaded the old house. How they had joked about ghosts and hauntings!

Marcia Wood stayed home from work, to be on hand in case the telephone rang. Althea and Ellen reluctantly went off to school, and Ben Wood drove to the police station, to make inquiries and to learn what he might do to help find his missing daughter.

Marcia Wood's presence in the house annoyed Ronald, creating as it did the need for continual vigilance. His mood was somewhat surly to begin with, since, like Barbara, he had not slept well.

After Ben Wood and the two girls had departed, Ronald closed off the peephole and turned on the light. He stood looking down at Barbara. What, really, did she think of him? She wasn't half as difficult as he had expected, and she actually seemed to enjoy the lovemaking. At least she said she did, and what could she gain by lying? Her notion of going off somewhere else was theoretically reasonable — but here was Atranta! And he might not like somewhere else, especially now that he had this delightful girl here for his very own... He bent down over the cot and kissed her. She could not bring herself to respond; she hated the feel of his facial hair. Ronald noticed and looked down in frowning suspicion. "What's the matter?" he whispered. "Is something wrong?"

"I don't like the rope around my neck," Barbara muttered.

"It's a necessary precaution. But I'll take it off. You've got to promise to be quiet."

"I'll be quiet."

Ronald untied the rope, which in any event got in the way of the lovemaking. "Is that better?"

Barbara rubbed her neck and nodded. Ronald bent forward and kissed her again. With her stomach jerking in anger and revulsion, Barbara forced herself to respond. Ronald's kissing became wet and passionate. Barbara let herself go limp, and Ronald proceeded with his lovemaking.

Meanwhile Barbara's mother washed the breakfast dishes, then went upstairs and made the beds.

At noon Ben Wood returned with a dark stocky man of forty-five: Sergeant Howard Shank from the County Sheriff's Office, whose voice was soft and polite in contrast to his expression of dyspeptic cynicism. Ronald instantly threw the loop around Barbara's neck and held the loose end wrapped around his hand; with a single jerk he could close off her windpipe. Barbara tried to protest, but Ronald refused to listen. "Maybe you wouldn't yell — but I can't be all that sure. I can't take any chances whatever!" He turned out the light and pressed his eye to the peephole.

"...unreasonable," Ben Wood was saying. "We're a close-knit family. It just doesn't make sense to any of us."

"That may be," said Shank. "Still, as you know, it happens all the time."

"Please don't make up your mind before you listen to us!" Marcia Wood declared. "We know Barbara! She was a sensible girl, a good girl!"

Shank gave a quizzical shrug. "What do you think happened?"

"I think someone drugged her, or frightened her, or threatened her — forced her to write that note — and then took her away."

"The handwriting is definitely hers?"

"Yes. Definitely."

Shank nodded dubiously. "I suppose such things happen. I haven't seen it myself. On the other hand, I've chased maybe five hundred girls who left home of their own free will. Sometimes a boy talks them into it. Sometimes they're bored, or their feelings are hurt. In fact, the note makes reference to a lack of trust. What's that all about?"

Ben and Marcia both compressed their lips: the same grimace at the same time. Shank thought that they even looked alike: both tall and spare with well-shaped if undistinguished features. Both were what he considered 'the salt of the earth' — and something about this 'lack of trust' phrase disturbed them.

Ben Wood said, "Some rather odd incidents occurred. We still can't explain them. A bottle of Ellen's perfume was spilled. Ellen is the oldest girl. Althea — she's the second one — keeps a diary which was broken into. The only person who might have been responsible is Barbara. She denied touching either the perfume or the diary — very vigorously, and of course we believed her, but there just wasn't anyone else to blame. So she felt we didn't trust her, which was nonsense... Since then, incidentally, we've taken to locking our house."

"I see," said Shank. "Barbara has a steady boyfriend?"

"No."

"Is she, well, boy-crazy?"

"I wouldn't say so. She likes attention, and because she's pretty she usually gets it. Basically she's a sensible girl."

"Does she smoke?"

"Never."

"No evidence of drugs?"

"Absolutely not."

"And she took nothing with her?"

"She left all her money and she went away — or was taken away — in her school clothes."

"I see." Shank rose to his feet. "Any recent photographs?"

"We've already given them to the local police, but they don't seem very interested."

"To be perfectly frank, there isn't much they can do. They've sent a bulletin out over the teletype, but once a kid gets to Berkeley or San Francisco, the ground swallows him up, and that's how it is unless he gets in trouble or decides to call home. It's a big problem for us, and I can't offer you too much encouragement."

Marcia Wood cried, "But we don't believe she ran away! We think she was kidnapped!"

Shank shrugged. "I'll make inquiries at her school. It's just possible she confided in one of her friends."

"We've already checked," said Ben Wood hollowly. "Nobody knows anything. In fact, she made plans to play tennis today."

Shank was impressed in spite of himself. With rather more vigor he said, "I'll do all I can to get a line on her. But I can't hold out too much hope."

Shank departed. Ben and Marcia Wood drank coffee in gloomy silence. Every idea, every theory had already been verbalized a dozen times.

In the lair Barbara lay taut with frustration. A half-dozen times she drew in her breath to scream and each time Ronald sensed her intent and gave the cord a menacing twitch. His amiability had disappeared.

He put his face close to her ear. "I know what you're thinking," he muttered. "Don't do it. You wouldn't live long enough to regret it. I don't have any worries. I've got a way to get out of here that you don't know about. If anybody broke in here they'd only find you, not me."

Barbara's throat was thick with woe; she could talk only with an effort. "Please don't hurt me, Ronald."

"You promised not to make any noise, and about five times you started to yell."

"No, no! I was just catching my breath. This rope is too tight!"

"It's tight on purpose. One good jerk is all it takes."

"Don't talk that way!" croaked Barbara.

"Sh! Not so loud!"

Barbara spoke in a husky whisper. "I thought we were going to be friends."

"I can't trust anybody."

"You could trust me! If you let me go, I could come in here every night! I could bring you ice cream and all kinds of good things. We could have lots of fun! Isn't that better than having me tied up like this?"

Ronald grinned. "No."

"But why not? Everything would be nicer, more exciting!"

"I wouldn't have you for myself. Now you're all mine."

"Then let's go off together. Let's go to Berkeley and live like the hippies do! No one would ever find us."

"No money."

"I could get money — some way. I'd work! Or even steal! Anything would be better than this little room."

"I don't know about that. This is Atranta."

"I'll bet if you wrote a book about Atranta you could sell it and make lots of money. You'd be famous, and I'd be proud of you!"

Ronald gave a ponderous nod. "I've considered that."

Barbara thought to discern a softening in his attitude. "I wouldn't mind leaving home. I'd like to — with you. You know how it's been around here — everybody accusing me of things I didn't do. And my parents are too strict. They don't let me do things I want to do. You and I could have such fun — but not here."

"I'm having fun now," said Ronald. "Aren't you?"

"Not always. I don't like that rope. It makes me nervous."

Ronald grinned. "That's the way I want it."

"Another thing — we don't have all that much food. And we don't have any way of getting more. Just think of the nice things we might have if we went somewhere else. Steaks and barbecued spareribs and hot dogs with mustard and fried chicken and french fries and milk shakes."

Ronald licked his lips. "It all takes money."

"We could go up to Lake Tahoe, and work at one of the hotels, or you could get a job at a service station."

"I don't like that kind of work."

"What kind of work do you like?"

"I don't know. I've never thought much about it. I'd like to be an artist, I guess."

"You certainly have the ability. Maybe there's an art school at Lake Tahoe. There must be lots of them in Berkeley."

"It all takes money."

Barbara said no more. Maybe one or another of these absurd ideas might seem sensible to Ronald, maybe she could lure him out into the open world. And then — how she'd run! Naked or clothed, it made no difference; she'd run down the street, through the middle of town — anywhere, so long as she was free!

She heard the telephone ring. Her mother answered. Barbara could not quite hear the conversation, but it seemed that someone at school had called. Her mother made a few polite but terse explanations, and ended the conversation as swiftly as possible.

Barbara meanwhile had a brilliant idea. "Ronald!"

"Sh! Not so loud! Don't talk like that again!"

Barbara pitched her voice at a lower level. "I just had a wonderful idea."

Ronald spoke in an austere whisper. "What kind of idea?"

"Well, you said we didn't have any money. I know how we can fix that problem."

"How?" Ronald's tone was indulgent, if skeptical.

"Suppose we hitchhiked, say, to Lake Tahoe, or Berkeley. I could telephone home and say I needed money for an emergency. I know my father and mother would send it to me." Barbara waited for Ronald's reaction. He said nothing. Barbara whispered eagerly, "Then we'd have enough money to live on."

Ronald whispered huskily, "I don't want to leave here."

"But why not? Think how nice the outside world is!"

Ronald grinned. "It's not real. Atranta is real. And Atranta is here."

"No, Ronald! Atranta is inside you! You'd take it with you, and be able to write beautiful stories, like the Oz books."

"They're for children," said Ronald disdainfully.

"No! Everybody reads them. And they made the author rich. You could be rich too. All you need to do is write about Atranta and draw beautiful illustrations. And I'd help you! I'd like to be rich too."

Ronald made a sound, half-sniff, half-snort. "What would you do?"

"Type. Keep house. Lots of things."

"Huh!" snorted Ronald. "Do you know something? I don't trust you."

Barbara was silent a moment. "Nothing I say seems to make any difference. I'd like to go live in Berkeley myself, or Mexico."

"They wouldn't let us past the border without passports."

"Arizona is another pretty place. My grandmother lives near Scottsdale. In fact — do you know something? We could go live with her. She's got a beautiful house, and she'd be glad to see us."

Ronald was superciliously amused, as if at the antics of a puppy. "She'd telephone your folks as soon as we arrived."

"I don't think she would, if I asked her not to. And suppose she called — so what? I'd tell my folks that I didn't want to come home for a while."

"Hmmf. Then what?"

"I don't know. Maybe Grandmother would help you get into an art school, if I asked her."

"Is she rich?" Ronald's interest was piqued.

"Oh yes, she's got lots of money."

Ronald turned away and lay staring up at the map on the ceiling.

Barbara held her breath. But Ronald said nothing. Barbara began to tremble. What would she do if Ronald saw through her pitiful artifices? Oh, what would she do? Something, somehow — but what? He was always too close upon her, always too suspicious. With a crawling stomach she twisted her face into an arch smile. "Aren't you hungry? I'd love a cheeseburger with french fries."

"Sh! Not so loud!"

"I think my mother's gone out."

"I didn't hear the door slam." Ronald listened. The house seemed silent, for a fact. He went to peer through his peepholes. During the few seconds his attention was distracted Barbara might have screamed, but if her mother actually had gone out who'd be there to hear? Even if her mother were home, before she figured out where the screaming came from, Ronald could do any dire deed he had in mind.

Ronald turned away from the dining room peephole. "She's writing a letter."

"To Grandmother probably."

Ronald had no great interest in the matter. He came back to sit on the cot, and began to touch Barbara — here, there, everywhere, rapt and marveling, as if even now he could hardly believe his wonderful good fortune. Barbara lay with a frozen face, then forced herself to relax; Ronald's distrust would feed upon any display of revulsion.

At four o'clock Ellen and Althea came home, and Marcia had to tell them that Barbara was still lost.

Dinner was silent and gloomy. The girls washed dishes, then did homework on the dining-room table. Ben and Marcia apathetically watched television.

About nine-thirty Ellen and Althea went upstairs to bed. An hour later Ben and Marcia followed. Ronald almost immediately opened the secret door and peered out into the pantry. He looked back at Barbara, and she could almost read his thoughts. He closed the door and said gruffly, "I'm going out for a minute or two, but first I'd better make things secure." He tied Barbara's ankles and wrists to the cot, and gagged her. Barbara lay rigid, chilled by the bleak conviction that Ronald was far too distrustful ever to venture forth from his lair, not to Berkeley, not to Tahoe: nowhere. All her coaxing and fawning had gone for naught. He might have given her proposals a languid theoretical consideration, but never would he risk the open world. Never.

Ronald went forth into the kitchen and returned with an onion, two slices of cold meat loaf, bread and butter, a cup of milk, two stalks of celery, a carrot, and a fair-sized serving of ice cream. This was more than his usual requisition, but now there were two mouths to feed, for a while, at least.

He untied Barbara, and sensed her despondency. It made no great difference one way or the other, but he spoke with brassy jocularity. "Look. Food! Yum-yum. Eat your ice cream first, before it gets cold."

"I'm not too hungry."

"Well, eat the carrot and some celery. Good for the complexion, you know."

"I don't care about my complexion." Tears began trickling down Barbara's face. "Ronald, please let me go. I don't want to stay in here any more. I feel all cramped and stuffy. Please let me go!"

Ronald, eating the ice cream, stared at her in astonishment. "You want to go? When we're having so much fun? It doesn't make sense!"

"I still want to go. Don't you want me to be happy?"

"Sure. I know how to make you happy."

"Then can I go? I'll tell my family that I decided to come home. I promise I won't tell about you being here. Really, Ronald. Please!"

Ronald frowned. "This doesn't make me feel very good. I thought we were starting to get along. You were full of ideas about Berkeley and Lake Tahoe and your grandmother. And now you want to leave."

"I just don't want to stay in here anymore. If you let me go, it would be better for both of us."

"Hah," said Ronald. "You'd tell your parents first thing."

"No, Ronald, I promise I wouldn't. And we can still be friends."

Ronald finished the ice cream. "You're so pretty — especially when you're all worked up. And you've got such a beautiful figure. You're cute all over."

"I appreciate the compliments, Ronald. But…"

"No more buts. Kiss me."

Barbara put her head on his shoulder. "After we do it, can I go?"

Ronald smilingly shook his head. "I enjoy your company too much."

"I'd see you every day, Ronald! After school I'm always home early!"

"Let's not talk."

Barbara sighed and drew a deep breath, fighting the almost overpowering pressure of hysteria. Ronald became busy and she lay inert, tears rolling down her cheeks.

Ronald at last removed his bulk. Barbara slid to the outside of the cot, disliking the constricted space between Ronald and the wall. Ronald made no protest, but sat watching her with heavy-lidded intensity. After a while he became drowsy, and his interest waned. His eyelids drooped. Barbara closed her own eyes, feigning sleep.

Ronald began to breathe in heavy regular gusts. Barbara slowly turned her head and looked toward the secret door. Twist the latch, raise the door, and slip through. She listened to Ronald's breathing. He was asleep.

Softly and carefully she moved: first one leg to the floor, then an arm. Ronald lay placid. Barbara eased off the cot: slowly, carefully. She took a step to the secret door; she bent and turned the latch. She lifted the door, and the hinges gave a little squeak. She froze for a half-second, then raised it high, and crawled through. A hand grasped her ankle. She heard Ronald's voice: a hissing guttural sound like nothing she had ever heard before. "You treacherous little bitch!"

Upstairs Ben Wood sat up in his bed. Marcia said, "Did you hear something?"

"I'd have sworn it was a scream."

"I heard it too. Or I thought I heard it. I was half-asleep."

"Do you know, it sounded like Babs."

Marcia said dubiously, "It was probably Ellen or Althea having a nightmare."

Ben jumped out of bed. He crossed to Ellen's room, opened the door. "Ellen? Are you all right?"

"Huh? What?"

"It's all right. Go back to sleep."

He checked Althea with the same result. He went to the head of the stairs, where he stood listening.

Silence.

He returned to the bedroom. "The girls were asleep... It must have been our imagination."

"It really *was* like Babs," said Marcia. "The sound rings in my ears."

Ben stood indecisive, wondering what he ought to do. Slowly he returned to bed. "For a fact it sounded like Babs... I suppose because she's so much in our minds... Some day she'll come back to us."

Marcia was crying. Ben put his arm around her and drew her close. Marcia said, "Wherever she is I hope she's not lonely or frightened."

Chapter XV

SATURDAY MORNING WAS DULL and damp. At nine o'clock rain began to fall. Ben and Marcia and the two girls sat late at the breakfast table. No one had slept well, and Althea complained of nightmares, which she couldn't quite remember. "I was off somewhere on a strange landscape. I couldn't see very well through the dark, but it seemed all stone and rock with the cold wind blowing — nowhere I've ever been. For some reason I had to walk along a trail and I didn't want to, but I had to…I remember the wind and voices calling from a far distance. And there was something before that, some terribly sad music, or maybe this was the wind." Althea shook her head. "I don't remember. It's so mixed up, but all so strange and sad."

Ben said, "It might have been…" then he stopped. "I looked in at you about midnight, and you seemed peaceful enough."

"Dreams are so strange," Ellen mused. "The psychologists say they represent fears and secret wishes. But I think they must be more than that."

"Primitive people think dreams are real," said Marcia. "They believe that the soul leaves the body."

Ben was not sympathetic to this point of view. "That's why they think that way: because they're primitive."

"Still, in things like that they know as much as we do."

"Maybe a lot more," said Althea.

Ben shook his head. "Not necessarily. For instance, a computer is much less complicated than a human brain, and computers get their circuits mixed up all the time. Savages don't know anything about computers or buggered circuits. All they know is what they see and feel, and they work out explanations based on what they know."

"Maybe our brains aren't computers," said Ellen softly. "Maybe they act like computers just often enough to fool the scientists."

"Hmmf," said Ben. "An awful lot of 'maybes'."

"I know that I've got at least two minds working all the time," said Althea. "Sometimes I relax the one on top just to see what the other one will do, and very interesting things happen. It's a lovely game to play when you've nothing better to do."

"That's how a lot of modern artists paint pictures," said Ben. "Unfortunately I'm not interested in their souls, any more than they're interested in mine."

"What is a 'soul'?" Ellen asked in an earnest voice. "Is there any such thing?"

Ben shrugged. "Some say 'yes', some say 'no'."

"So many odd things happen," said Althea. "Things no one can explain."

Marcia sighed, and changed the subject. "Is there a football game today? It'll be miserable in all this wet."

"The game's at Barnett," said Ellen. "I don't want to go. Especially not in the rain."

"Where's all the school spirit?" asked Ben with a wan attempt at facetiousness.

Ellen smiled her half-rueful smile. "I'm a refugee from Los Gatos High. I'm just attending classes here to get my diploma."

"I'm not going to the game either," said Althea. "I plan to stay home and read *Titus Groan*."

"You're going to read *what*?" asked Ben Wood.

"*Titus Groan*. It's a book about a strange old castle and the people who live there. I'm rather like Fuchsia, I think. She's a beautiful solitary girl who likes to brood in the attic where the Groans keep all their old junk."

"You and Fuchsia would make a good pair," said Ben. "Both odd-balls."

"Sulky-sweet Fuchsia."

"What happens to her?" asked Ellen.

"I don't know. I'm only halfway through the book."

"During Christmas vacation I'm going to read *Remembrance of*

Things Past," said Ellen. "I absolutely intend to do so, no matter who laughs at me."

Ben Wood gave a sad chuckle, but made no remark. Everyone knew where his thoughts had been wandering. Two weeks previously the family had made tentative plans to visit Arizona during the Christmas vacation. Now, with Barbara gone, the trip was unthinkable.

At noon Ben and Marcia went out to shop for groceries. Duane Mathews telephoned and half an hour later arrived in person. Ellen made grilled-cheese sandwiches and hot chocolate, and the three ate lunch at the dining-room table. Duane had quit his job at the service station and was at loose ends. He spoke rather despondently of the pressures being put on him by his family. "Dad wants me to work at the bar. He'll put in a pizza oven if I'm willing to take charge of it. I'd make lots of money, and get the whole business when Dad retires. My mother wants me to go to college and learn something. And me — I don't know what I want to do. I'm not anxious to be a pizza cook — still I suppose it's just work."

"I thought you wanted to be a veterinarian," said Althea, subtly seeming to suggest that between the crafts of fabricating pizzas and ministering to sick dogs there was little choice.

"That's my mother's idea. My Uncle Ed's a veterinarian in Lodi. He's got a big house with a swimming pool and a Lincoln Continental. He and my aunt fly to Europe every year. There's lots of money in that racket for sure."

"What about you?" asked Ellen. "You must have a preference."

Duane drummed his fingers on the tabletop. "Oh yes. No question about that. I want to be a criminologist."

"A criminologist?" Althea raised her eyebrows. "Whatever for?"

"The field is obviously wide open. When Ronald Wilby could murder my sister and get away scot-free, somewhere there's a lack."

"What exactly did the police do?" asked Ellen.

"Routine. They put out an alert and asked Mrs. Wilby a few questions. They checked the bus station and asked if anyone had seen Ronald hitchhiking, and that was about the end of it."

"What else could they do?" Althea asked. "For instance, what would you have done?"

"His mother knew where Ronald went. She wasn't the type not to know, and Ronald wasn't the type to go off without mama giving him a lot of help. She must have sent him money. That's the angle I would have worked on. I'd have watched her mail, and I'd have checked on what she did with her money, because she worked herself to death, no question about it, and why? To get money for Ronald."

"That's just suspicion," said Ellen. "How could you prove it?"

"I don't know." Duane reflected a moment, then said almost grudgingly, "It doesn't make too much difference now anyway, because the woman is dead. If I'd been a police detective I'd have nailed her. Sure as anything, she helped Ronald get away!"

Althea said in a musing voice, "Still, you've got to feel sorry for her. She probably suffered as much as your own mother. Maybe more."

Duane gave a bleak nod. "That's what Mom said herself. I don't doubt it. Still, what's right is right, and she should have turned Ronald over to the police."

Ellen reflected a moment. "Would you protect your son if he committed a crime?"

"I'd turn him in," said Duane. "I wouldn't like it, but that's what I'd do. Mrs. Wilby was a silly, selfish woman. She was all wrapped up in that horrible Ronald, and it killed her when he went wrong."

Ellen and Althea sat in silence for a moment or two. The telephone rang. Ellen ran into the living room and picked up the receiver. "Hello... Yes, he's still here... Art's Service Station. I'll ask him." She came back to the dining room. "Mom and Dad need a lift. The fuel pump has gone out on the station wagon."

Duane rose to his feet. "I know where Art's is. Tell 'em we'll be right there."

Ellen and Duane departed. Althea went to sprawl on the sofa with her book.

The house seemed very silent. Althea put her book down and lay listening to the rain. She began to wish she'd gone with Duane and Ellen, but no one would be in the house in case Barbara telephoned. How wonderful it would be if Barbara actually did call, from Berkeley, or San Francisco, to say that she wanted to come home. How happy everyone would be! Althea concentrated upon a thought: *Come home,*

Babs, come home!... At least telephone, let us know where you are!... Babs, Babs, Babs! Where are you?

She lay passive, receptive, hoping for connection...Nothing. At least, nothing very much. She felt dampness and heard sighing winds: a residue, so she decided, of last night's nightmare. *Babs! Babs!* thought Althea. *Come home, come home! We love you and miss you!* And Althea lay with her eyes closed, holding her mind blank.

"I can't."

Althea opened her eyes with a startled jerk. The words had come in small crystalline vibrations, and it seemed like Barbara's voice.

Babs! Babs! thought Althea. *Do you hear me? Is that you? Why can't you come home?*

Silence, except the rain, the ticking of the clock, a creaking of woodwork from the direction of the kitchen. In Althea's mind: nothing but darkness, the blowing of the dream-wind, a slow seep of the most melancholy desolation imaginable.

Althea's concentration had frayed; she relaxed her attention. Suddenly the old house seemed full of strange noises. Althea became uneasy. Irrational, she told herself with a contemptuous little laugh for her own foolishness. But she sat up on the sofa, then rose to her feet, and went to the front door. Strange, the sounds in the old house!

Althea went out to stand on the porch.

The rain came quietly down; the air was soft and cool. Althea felt more at ease. The air inside had been oppressive. Perhaps someone had set the thermostat too high. She shivered. The air was somewhat too cool. Perhaps the house would now feel less warm. She tried the door to discover that she had locked herself out, and so she had to wait five minutes until her parents arrived home in Duane's car.

Days went by. The Woods settled into a new and rather despondent way of life. No one spoke of Barbara, though every mealtime her empty place brought recollection. On Saturday Ben and Marcia drove into Berkeley. They gave no explanation, but Ellen and Althea understood that they intended to look for Barbara, and that they would leave messages at the various agencies which helped strays and runaways.

Duane Mathews dropped by the house at eleven o'clock with a

package of pork chops and a loaf of French bread. "Instead of you feeding me," he told the girls, "I'm going to cook lunch for you."

"Pork chops for lunch?" asked Althea.

"Nope. Barbecued-pork sandwiches. I should have brought some potato salad."

"Let's make some," said Ellen. "It won't take long."

"You two can be in charge of the potato salad. Then this afternoon maybe we'll drive over to Steamboat Slough. There's a boat at Pete's Landing I want to look at."

"I can't come," said Althea. "I promised to help Bernice with her costume."

"I can't come either," said Ellen. "I've got a report to write. 'The Reasons for Hamlet's Indecisiveness'."

"It's been done," said Duane.

"Not the way I'm doing it. I've got a new approach. If Hamlet is decisive the play only goes three scenes."

"It's original scholarship, but you might not get much of a grade."

"I don't care all that much. I'm so bored with school. The hell with the report, I'd rather go to Steamboat Slough."

"First the potato salad," said Althea. "I'll peel potatoes. You can chop the onions."

"Thanks."

"I'll chop onions," said Duane. "I need some for the barbecue sauce."

Ellen went into the pantry. "How many?"

"Just one, and whatever you need for the salad."

"There's only three left," said Ellen. "Somebody around here likes onions. Mom just bought a big bag last week. We'll need potatoes—they're almost gone too! I guess there's enough. Just barely…We're out of everything, as usual."

Duane browned the pork chops and simmered them at low heat in barbecue sauce; meanwhile the potatoes boiled.

"What would go well with this meal is beer," said Duane. "In fact, I've got a six-pack out in the car."

"Bring it in," said Ellen. "I love beer!"

"Well—I don't want your parents to think I'm corrupting their daughters."

"That's locking the barn door after the horses are gone," said Althea.

"I can't remember not being corrupt," said Ellen.

"Well, all right, if you're sure they won't be upset."

"Not a chance."

The three had departed. The house was silent.

The pantry sounded to a barely audible scrape. In the shadows a bulky shape stood erect. Ronald came slowly out into the kitchen. His nose drew him to the stove. Duane had cooked generously; in the pan remained a quantity of barbecued pork and ample sauce.

Detesting Duane as he did, Ronald stood glowering a moment or two, then tearing off a chunk of French bread, he smeared it thick with margarine and got to work on the pork. He remembered the potato salad, and opening the refrigerator, served himself a great mound: the girls wouldn't remember whether a gallon had been left or a cupful. It was the best meal he'd had in days! He finished it off with a portion of vanilla ice cream swimming in chocolate sauce, topped with a sliced banana, chopped nuts and a huge squirt of synthetic whipped cream. Delicious beyond words, thought Ronald. Regretfully he decided against a second helping, and cleaned up the evidence of his repast. Then he went into the living room and stood by the window.

Bernice and Wallace Thurston were the daughter and son of the Methodist minister. Althea suspected that the old adage about clergymen's children held true. Nothing too outrageous had ever occurred in her presence; nevertheless, they generated an atmosphere of excitement and mischief which made for interesting company. Althea found Wallace attractive, and he seemed to like her too, and she was hoping he'd ask for a date. Today she'd flirt as well as she knew how, and try not to scare him off with her intelligence.

Today luck was against her. Bernice's piano teacher had switched schedules and Bernice had a three o'clock lesson. Mrs. Thurston did not care to leave Wallace and Althea alone in the house so on the way to the piano lesson she dropped Althea off at home.

Althea, somewhat miffed at Mrs. Thurston's fastidious propriety, hoped that Wallace would telephone; she had even hinted as much.

In the meantime she'd fix her fingernails and do some reading for her English class.

The key was in its usual place. She opened the door and went into the house.

At five o'clock Duane and Ellen returned from Steamboat Slough. The house seemed empty. On the dining-room table Ellen found a note.

Dear Everybody:

While you were gone I heard from Barbara, and I'm going to talk to her. I promised I wouldn't tell where she is, so I can't divulge any details.

Don't worry about me; I'll be fine.

Love, Althea

CHAPTER XVI

"I DON'T BELIEVE IT," said Ellen. "I just don't believe it!"

Duane snatched up the letter and glared at it, as if to compel further information from the cryptic sentences. "If Althea learned where Barbara was, would she keep the news a secret — no matter what she promised? Would you?"

"No," said Ellen. "I don't think I would. I don't think she did either."

"Oh? Why do you say that?"

"Notice the handwriting."

"What about it? Isn't it Althea's?"

"Oh it's Althea's handwriting all right. But it's backhand. She doesn't write like that."

Duane again inspected the note. "What time will your folks be home?"

"I don't know. I expect they'll make a day of it."

"You'd better call the police."

Ellen telephoned the Oakmead Police Department and reported Althea's disappearance. She told Duane, "They're not too pleased."

"I imagine not. They haven't even found the other one yet. Who lives next door?"

"The Schumachers and Boltons."

"Let's go talk to them."

Ronald turned away from the wall and directed a haughty glance down at Althea. "So — you tried to trick me. You disguised your handwriting."

Althea said nothing.

Ronald opened his mouth to say something sarcastic, then thought better of it; why bother? None of these girls could be trusted; they said one thing and meant another. Still, he had not expected any such cheap treachery from Althea; he thought somehow she might be different. But she was far more cold and tense than Barbara, and she hadn't so much as mentioned the Atranta pictures.

Well, so be it. If she wasn't nice to him, he wasn't going to be nice to her. That was the way the world went, and she might as well find it out sooner than later. He spoke in an important voice, combining exactly the proper degrees of dignity and silken menace, "Please don't try to play any more tricks on me."

Neither the Schumachers nor the Boltons had so much as noticed Althea's arrival home.

Ellen telephoned the Thurston house. Wallace answered. "Althea? She left for home about three with Mother and Bernice. Isn't she there now?"

"I guess she went downtown." Ellen hung up and turned back to Duane. "She left the Thurston's about three."

"So now it's five. She could be anywhere by now…I know that message isn't right. But just on the off chance it is, we ought to go out to the highway and look for her. If she's hitchhiking she might still be there."

"Althea wouldn't hitchhike. She wouldn't ride ten feet with a stranger. Just a minute." She ran upstairs and into Althea's room, then returned downstairs rather more slowly. "Her money is still there."

"Just like Barbara's money."

The police arrived. They examined the note and listened to everything Ellen had to tell them. "So you don't think the note is genuine?"

"I know it isn't genuine. The handwriting is backwards and it doesn't sound like Althea. It's not the way she talks or thinks."

The police officer gave a skeptical nod. "Well, I'll put the word out over the wire. Where are your folks?"

"They went to Berkeley to look for Barbara."

"And while they're gone, another one disappears. Great." The officer examined the letter. "I suppose you've had your hands all over this?"

"Well — yes. We didn't think of fingerprints."

"Hmmf. Ordinary typing paper."

Duane had became restive. He asked, "Isn't there something you can do, instead of just standing here asking questions?"

"Sonny, if I could figure out something to do, I'd do it. All I can think of is that the first girl went off to one of those hippie communes along the river, and the other girl went to keep her company. I can check these places out, and, as I say, we'll put a bulletin out on the wire."

"That's just wasted effort! Somebody kidnapped her, just like they kidnapped Barbara!"

"Well, I suppose that's possible, and I'll take it up with Captain Davis. We'll sure do our best."

The police departed. The house seemed bleak and cold and silent. Ellen began to sob. Duane put his arm around her and patted her hand. "Oh Duane, what are we going to do? I can't bear to tell Mom and Daddy!"

"Let's go out and look for her," Duane growled. "It's better than standing here doing nothing. Leave a note. Tell them we'll be back as soon as we can."

Ellen scribbled a note and left it on the dining-room table along with Althea's message; the two of them ran out the front door and the house was again silent.

Ronald relaxed the noose around Althea's neck. "We can talk now, but quietly. First of all, don't be so scared. I'm not going to bite you. All you have to do is obey orders! And that means no noise! no rumpus! no yelling! Do you understand?" Ronald raised his voice a menacing degree or two. "I said, do you understand?"

Althea nodded. In a husky whisper she asked, "Where is Barbara?"

Ronald smiled: a lordly condescending smile. "She was here until she got bored. One night when you were all asleep she ran away. She said she was going to Lake Tahoe. She wanted to play around a bit before coming home."

"What about me?" Althea quavered. "What are you going to do with me?"

"Don't worry about that," said Ronald. "After a while you can leave — if you promise to keep my secret."

"Then let me go now! Please!"

Ronald smilingly shook his head. "We've got lots of things to talk about. Barbara wasn't much of a talker."

Althea stared at him numbly. She blurted, "Who are you?" But even as she asked, knowledge burst into her brain. This was Ronald Wilby. Ronald Wilby the murderer!

Ronald replied in a gentle, almost mincing, voice, "My name is beside the point. Just call me Norbert." He made a gesture around the walls. "What do you think of the atmosphere in here?"

Althea gave the decorations an uncomprehending glance. "Won't you let me go? Please! I don't want to stay here!"

Ronald's eyebrows lowered into a majestic frown. Althea saw that she had taken the wrong line.

"You'll stay here until I see fit to let you go," said Ronald. "And let's get one thing understood. You'd better behave yourself. I'm good-natured, but I can't take chances. One squeak out of you when anyone is in the house, and I'd have to jerk that noose…Watch!" Ronald tugged on the loose end of the rope. The noose became an overhand knot, barely large enough to push a finger through. Althea stared aghast.

Barbara had been more tractable, more quickly comprehending, thought Ronald. She also had shown less obstinacy and, well, call it nervousness, even though she was younger. Althea was still fully dressed. It would be fun taking off her clothes, one piece at a time. But first, he must make absolutely sure she knew what was required of her. In an easy conversational tone he asked, "So now do you understand what will happen if you make any noise?"

Althea only stared at him, like a person bereft of reason.

Ronald spoke a bit more meaningfully. "Please, tell me that you understand what I'm talking about."

Althea managed a nod. Ronald relaxed. "Actually, I want to be friends with you," he said. "We'll be living here together until you decide you want to leave —"

"I want to leave now!"

"— and I decide to let you go."

Althea whispered, "Tell me where Barbara is."

"I already told you. She's gone up to Lake Tahoe. At least that's where she said she was going. She promised she wouldn't tell about me, and I guess she kept her promise. You'll have to do the same thing."

Althea began to cry. "I'll promise not to tell. But let me go now! Please be kind to me! I don't want to stay in here!"

"Too bad," said Ronald with a grim smirk. "You'll like it after a while."

Althea shook her head. "Don't you realize you'll be in bad trouble when the police catch you?"

"*If* the police catch me — which is not likely. I've been here for — well, it's been a long time. I've been writing the history of Atranta. Aren't you interested?"

"I don't know anything about it."

"It's a magical country. Those men," Ronald pointed, "they're the six dukes, and those are their castles. The girl is Fansetta. I didn't do the best job with her. Maybe you'll pose for me. She's supposed to look about like you." Ronald improvised the last remark, but it was quite true. Barbara never had quite fit the image; she was too fresh-faced and alert. Althea had more of a thoughtful fairy-quality to her; she was obviously more sensitive and imaginative, and perhaps more passionate. Barbara's reactions hadn't been all that exciting; she had just lain there. Ronald cocked his head. "Someone's coming." He tied the noose around her neck, with one end made fast to the stud, and the other wrapped around his hand. "Remember! Not a single sound. Or you won't like what happens."

Althea closed her eyes, and let the tears well out from under the lids. Barbara at Lake Tahoe? If only it were true! She shivered, and Ronald threw her a monitory glance. "Quiet," he hissed.

Ben and Marcia Wood came into the house, hungry, haggard, tired, and out of sorts. They read the two notes and stared at each other in despair. Ben stalked into the living room and telephoned the police, who assured him that all possible steps were being taken. Ben wanted to rave and threaten and bluster, but could think of nothing sensible to say.

Ellen and Duane presently returned, Ellen sagging with discouragement, Duane seething with quiet rage. Far into the night they all sat at the dining-room table, forming bewildered hypotheses. Duane went home at half-past eleven; Ellen went with him out on the porch. Duane kissed her and held her close for a moment, and Ellen, who had never encouraged Duane to be demonstrative, relaxed and allowed herself to be comforted. Duane whispered fiercely, "Promise me one thing! That no matter what, you won't go off looking for Barbara or Althea without telling me."

"I promise," said Ellen.

"No matter what!"

"No matter what."

"There's something awfully strange going on," Duane muttered. "If I had any brains I'd be able to figure it out. After all, I'm the one who wants to be a criminologist."

Ellen stirred. "I'd better go back inside — or Mom and Dad will start worrying about me."

The next day was Sunday. Ben Wood telephoned the Sheriff's office. Howard Shank had the day off and Ben Wood left a message. An hour later Shank returned the call and Ben reported Althea's disappearance. "We find it simply incredible," Ben declared. "Althea definitely and positively would not have gone off alone. Even less than Barbara."

"Even if Barbara had telephoned and asked her to come?"

"She'd certainly have given us more facts."

"Read the note again."

Ben Wood did so. Shank asked, "I suppose everybody in the house has handled the letter?"

"I'm afraid so."

"And she left her money behind?"

"She took nothing whatever, except the clothes she wore to her friend's house."

"Hmm. This is an unusual situation, I agree…Well, I'd better drive on out."

Ben Wood gave a shaky laugh. "I know how you must value your time off, but we're at wit's end."

"I'll get the time back."

Howard Shank arrived. He looked into Althea's room; he walked around the house seeking traces and clues; he drove to the Reverend Thurston's house and put inquiries to both Wallace and Bernice. Next he visited the Schumachers and the Boltons, and then Kathy Schmidt and Ernestine Long: girls with whom Althea was friendly. Everywhere he encountered a vacuum of information. Everyone presented about the same picture of Althea: a quietly happy girl, if over-imaginative and somewhat dreamy. No one considered her either adventurous or particularly decisive, and no one could take seriously the proposition that Althea would voluntarily leave her home unless forced to do so by some awful emergency — which neither the text of her letter nor its tone suggested.

"On these premises," Shank told the Woods, "we've got to assume that she's been kidnapped."

"That's what I told you when Barbara went!" Ben Wood rasped in a suddenly harsh voice. "The same thing has happened to both of them!"

Shank said stonily, "Perhaps you were right. We never discounted the idea either. But the fact remains that we had no leads. Without straw we can't make bricks. I can't search every house, barn, shed, church, garage, and motel in San Joaquin County."

"What about sex offenders?" Marcia asked.

"We've checked our list," said Shank. "Oakmead's pretty clean. The only sex criminal of recent years was Ronald Wilby, and he lived in this very house."

"And you've never caught him."

Shank shook his head. "Like Barbara and Althea, he simply disappeared."

"I wonder if there could be some connection."

Shank considered the proposition. "Well — nothing's impossible. That's one thing you learn in this business. Still, is it reasonable that Ronald Wilby should come back to Oakmead, where almost certainly he'd be recognized? It doesn't make much sense. There's nothing here for him now with his mother dead."

"Maybe so. But I just don't believe in coincidences."

"They happen all the time."

Marcia suggested, "Why don't we ask the newspapers to print pictures of the girls? And we'd offer a reward for information."

"It won't do any harm," said Shank. "Let me make the arrangements. I can get faster action."

"I keep coming back to this Ronald Wilby," said Ben Wood. "Does he have any friends or relatives in the area who might hide him?"

"No friends we were ever able to locate. None of his relatives are local people, and they all disown him."

Marcia gave a quavering cry of frustration and beat her fists on the table. "It's the same old story. No one knows anything, no one does anything. And meanwhile what's happening to our girls? It's enough to drive me absolutely crazy."

"I sympathize with you, Mrs. Wood. Please believe we'll do everything possible. Let me look at those notes again."

Marcia brought them forth, and Shank studied them for several minutes, then said, "The notes are either genuine — or they're not. If they're genuine, we've got to look for two silly wayward girls."

"They're not silly, and they're not wayward."

Shank nodded. "If the notes are not genuine, if the girls were forced to write them as you suspect, then we've got a very ugly situation on our hands. But — I won't try to fool you — I just don't see any starting point to the case. We've got to hope for some kind of break. Meanwhile, we'll make inquiries everywhere feasible. The city police have suggested that we look into the communes along the river, which is a long shot at best. Still, who knows?" Shank rose to his feet. He studied the notes one last time. "I'll take these along with me, if you don't mind."

Ben Wood made a weary gesture. "Go ahead. We know them by heart."

Ronald listened attentively to the conversation. As always, he deeply resented the terms 'sex offender', 'deviate', 'murderer' when used in connection with himself. Such words simply didn't fit the case; they implied a vulgar ordinary criminality which Ronald was far above and beyond.

So far neither Barbara nor Althea had correctly fulfilled their roles. Barbara had suggested going off to more spacious quarters in Berkeley or at Lake Tahoe; she had naturally been trying to hoodwink him, and obviously had never accepted the ambience of magic Atranta. Ronald had expected more subtlety and awareness of Althea. During the night he had spoken at length of Atranta. He had recounted its history and described the landscapes; he had limned the persons of each of the six dukes and taken her room by room through each of the six castles. He told of bewitching Fansetta and her marvelous adventures, of Mersilde and the halfling Darrue, and he kept watching her covertly, hoping to discern a gleam of interest. But Althea lay apathetic, and indeed the only time she evinced any sort of emotion was when Ronald proposed a session of lovemaking, whereupon she winced and shuddered and withdrew into numbness like a hermit crab into a shell. Barbara had been braver, more matter-of-fact; Althea seemed to regard each coition as a new and separate outrage: a fact which began to stimulate in Ronald a darker, more intricate, pleasure. Althea could not be aroused to passion, but she could be shocked and revolted, and Ronald began to plan a series of variations by which he could constantly stimulate her to awareness, the hard way.

Althea had nothing to say. She lay either silently staring, or torpid and dazed. Ronald became exasperated. He wanted her attention, her wonder, her awe; after all, she was Althea, who loved fantasies! He had opened before her the wonderful vistas of Atranta, and she lay like a half-wit!

On several occasions Althea aroused herself to plead with Ronald. She offered him inducements to let her go free. She swore never to reveal his secret; she undertook to give him money, if only he'd let her go. Ronald listened with a pursy noncommittal smile. When she asked how long he intended to keep her, he said, "Heavens, we've only got started!" And another time, "Time to talk about that when we're bored with each other. I find you entrancing. You have more feeling than Barbara. She was a practical girl."

" 'Was'?" asked Althea in a throaty whisper.

Ronald made an easy response. "While she was here. I guess she's still the same, wherever she is."

"But why did she go?" Althea insisted, trying to keep the quaver from her voice. "Why didn't she just come back to the family?"

Ronald's reply was glib and unconcerned. "Because I made her promise not to tell about me. She thought that if she went to Lake Tahoe she could call home and no one would suspect she'd been in the house all that time."

Althea tried to trace the thread of the argument, and discerned a certain weird rationality. Still, why would Barbara delay so long? Althea thought better of putting the question to Ronald.

As for the lovemaking, she recognized that he enjoyed making her squirm, but unlike Barbara, who had borne Ronald's exertions with stoicism, she could not conceal her repugnance. Her refuge was the feigned torpor which Ronald found so irksome. Meanwhile through half-closed lids she studied every detail of the lair and its contents. No question but what Ronald had a real flair for mood and grotesque detail; under different circumstances she might even have become interested in his contrivings. But now her preoccupation was escape, and she calculated a dozen schemes to this end.

Ronald was wary. With anyone downstairs he gagged her and tightened the noose so she could barely breathe, and she recognized that never could she call for help — unless Ronald became careless.

She studied the layout of the lair and saw how the old doorway had been sheathed with plasterboard. Given five seconds she might be able to hurl herself at this plasterboard and break through into the hall — but more likely she'd find her strength unequal to the task. Even while Ronald slept he seemed alert. Once or twice she stirred and tried to sit up; instantly he was awake and suspicious.

The trapdoor to the crawl-space she noticed but failed to identify. She saw no opportunity to escape.

Could she incapacitate Ronald? Could she poison him, or stun him, or stab him?

For poison, she saw only the watercolors, which probably weren't toxic. She searched in vain for a sharp object which might serve as a weapon. Ronald's two knives were both ordinary tableware, and the forks were equally useless. In all the lair she noted but one object which might be used as a weapon: the porcelain lid to the tank behind the toilet. Such objects, in her experience, were hard to lift free without producing a sepulchral clanking sound. Still, with great care it was surely possible.

When she went to the toilet she took careful note of how Ronald disposed himself. If anyone were in the house he usually sat on the edge of the cot, somewhat turned away from her; when the house was empty or late at night he often remained sprawled on the cot.

Yes, thought Althea; the deed was possible. Quite possible. She began to rehearse the procedure; she accomplished the act over and over in her mind. She'd need all her strength, all her courage, all her decisiveness — because she'd only have one chance.

Success probably depended upon two circumstances. No, three. Could she lift the cover silently? Would Ronald divine her intentions before she could strike the blow? Did she possess sufficient strength to do the job properly?

She thought 'yes' for the first and third situations, and she hoped 'no' for the second.

On Tuesday, pictures of Barbara and Althea Wood appeared in newspapers all over the state. The captions typically read,

> Have you seen either of these two girls? $1,000 reward is offered for information as to their whereabouts. Mr. Ben Wood of Oakmead, in San Joaquin County, believes his two daughters have been kidnapped. Both have disappeared under mysterious circumstances. Please communicate any information directly to the police. Barbara is 13, with blonde hair of medium length and blue eyes. She was last seen wearing a gray skirt and a dark-red turtleneck blouse. Althea is 16, with light brown hair, gray eyes, and was last seen wearing blue jeans and a green sweater.

Duane Mathews sat in the living room with Ellen. The photographs, so they agreed, were good likenesses and might well produce results — if the girls had appeared anywhere in public.

Duane was pessimistic. "I don't think there's a chance. I hate to say this, but ..." He could not bring himself to continue.

Ellen failed to notice; her thoughts ran concurrently with his.

"Somehow we should be able to figure something out," said Duane. "These things can't just happen without leaving a trace — but where's the trace?"

Ellen gave her head a weary shake. "We've been over it and over it. There's nothing but the notes."

"Could it be that somewhere in the notes is information we haven't understood? A hidden clue?"

Ellen gave a sad laugh. "You're letting your criminological instincts run away with you."

"Still," said Duane, "let's consider the notes and try to think like Sherlock Holmes."

"Sergeant Shank has the notes," said Ellen. "But I know them word for word."

She went to the desk and, bringing out two sheets of paper, wrote the two messages.

> *Dear Everybody:*
>
> *Nobody trusts me and I can't stand it anymore. I've gone off to join the hippies. I'll be back after a while. Don't worry about me. I'll be all right.*
>
> *Barbara*

> *Dear Everybody:*
>
> *While you were gone I heard from Barbara, and I'm going to talk to her. I promised I wouldn't tell where she is, so I can't divulge any details.*
>
> *Don't worry about me; I'll be fine.*
>
> *Love, Althea*

Sitting side by side on the couch, Duane and Ellen scrutinized the two messages.

"First of all," said Duane, "both notes are short, and both start off 'Dear Everybody'. Would you expect that?"

"I suppose so. It seems natural."

"Barbara's note mentions 'trust' — which refers to your private quarrels." Duane sat frowning at the word. "It occurs to me that's significant! No outsider would have known anything about that."

Ellen nodded slowly. "Well — I suppose you could argue that way."

"It's obvious! Would she have discussed the quarrel, or misunderstanding, whatever it was, with anybody you can think of?"

"No. But there's something else which makes an outsider certain."

"Oh? What?"

"The paper."

"The paper? There wasn't anything strange about the paper."

"I know. It was ordinary cheap typing paper. Just now I thought about it. Feel this paper here. It's good quality paper, telephone company paper. Daddy brings it home from his office. Larcenous Daddy. We never buy typing paper. That other paper was brought into the house — by an outsider."

Duane inspected the paper with scowling intensity. "Are you absolutely sure?"

"Absolutely. I'll show you." Ellen led him to the desk and displayed the contents. "Whenever we want a sheet of paper this is where we come. I don't have any such paper in my room. Let's go check the other bedrooms — just to make sure."

As Ellen had affirmed, no paper similar to that of the notes could be found in the house.

Duane said, "This is absolutely fascinating. Barbara's message almost guarantees that no outsider dictated it, but neither Barbara nor Althea would have had that paper to write on, unless an outsider gave it to them."

"But there's no outsider who knew of our quarrel with Barbara, except maybe you."

Duane laughed weakly. "I didn't do it."

"I think we ought to tell Sergeant Shank about the letters," said Ellen. "It's something I'm sure he hasn't thought of."

"Call him."

Ellen found Howard Shank at his desk, and explained the paradox she and Duane had discovered. Shank agreed that the contradiction was most perplexing. "It certainly bears out the idea that the girls didn't go off by themselves. Who could have known of the quarrel, other than members of the family?"

"Well — Duane might have known. But when Althea disappeared he was with me. I know Duane isn't responsible."

"I see. And he's there with you now?"

"Yes, he is. He's had innumerable opportunities to kidnap me but he doesn't seem to want to."

"Don't take the pitcher to the well too often," said Shank. "Have you told your parents about these letters?"

"No. Mom's shopping and Dad's at work. They'll be home any time now. I'll tell them when they come in. Have you had any results from the photographs?"

"Nothing definite. I'll keep you informed."

Ronald stood with his eye to the peephole. The detestable Duane! Never had he hated anyone with such virulence, not even Jim Neale. Duane wouldn't let anything rest; he kept nagging at things. What business was it of his about those notes? For the first time Ronald felt a trifle insecure. Because the only possible synthesis of ideas to explain the paradox of the letters would be this: an outsider, situated where he could overhear the quarrel, had provided the paper and kidnapped the girls. The next question would be: where was this outsider situated? That detestable rotten Duane!

Ronald sat on the cot. Althea turned away her head. Ronald frowned. Something was on her mind. She was brooding. Let her brood. He reached out, fondled her body. She was about an inch taller than Barbara and just a bit more slender and flexible. Her hips were more boyish than Barbara's, but she was probably more enticing, because of her sensitivity. Ronald rather liked doing things to revolt her…She had beautiful eyes, not blue like Barbara's, but gray like storm clouds, large and transparent. She had a beautiful mouth, and he liked to kiss her, because she always pulled her wrist across her mouth afterwards. Once a hair from his beard got caught in her teeth.

The evening passed. Ronald listened to the dinner-table discussion, which he found uninteresting. He'd heard it all before.

For dinner the Woods had brought home a paper bucket of fried chicken with french fries and coleslaw, and a frozen coconut custard pie. Everything looked most appetizing and Ronald hoped there'd be leftovers. Unfortunately, with the gluttonous Duane on hand, the chicken and french fries were totally consumed, and Ronald knew that tonight his mouth had watered in vain. There would be quite a bit of pie left, however: dessert for himself and Althea.

Duane went home at ten o'clock, and a half-hour later the three

Woods went upstairs to bed. Ronald stood by the toilet, ready to flush it as soon as someone upstairs did so. Now! Perfect synchronization, as usual.

He came back to the cot. Althea closed her eyes and turned to lie facing away from him. Ronald refused to take the hint, and busied himself.

The first event of the evening accomplished, Ronald sat up. Now for supper. Althea lay limp, humiliated. She'd perk up with a nice piece of pie and a cup of coffee and whatever else he could find. Ronald went briskly to the secret door. He hesitated, looked back. He had neglected to tie and gag Althea — but she'd hardly dare make a sound. He was really hungry and impatient to get to the refrigerator. He'd chance it this once.

He got down on his hands and knees, then chanced to look back over his shoulder. Althea was watching him with a peculiarly alert expression... Ronald drew back, slowly rose to his feet. He'd better not take any chances; no telling what kind of mischief Althea had worked up. She was cunning and merciless and she hated him; this he knew. All of which made for excitement and stimulation and lots of novel schemes, but he could never think of her as trustworthy.

"Sorry," said Ronald with a rather unctuous smirk, "but I think I'd better make all secure before I leave."

Althea's face drooped. She had a plan all worked out; if Ronald ever left her alone for even two minutes, she'd take the toilet lid and break through the plasterboard which covered the old doorway; then, if Ronald tried to come at her through the secret door, she'd hit him on the head.

Ronald, sensing her mood, tied and gagged her with especial care, then ducked out through his secret door and hurried to the refrigerator. As he had feared, nothing much was available except the pie. Hissing in irritation he cut two pieces. Not too much of the pie remained, but the Woods, preoccupied with their problems, would never notice. He poured leftover coffee into a pair of cups and returned into the lair.

Althea, when untied, accepted the coffee, but refused the pie. "I don't feel well."

"Oh? That's too bad," said Ronald. "I'm sorry to hear that." Sitting on the end of the cot he ate both pieces of pie, and regretfully gave over the idea of going back to the refrigerator for what was left. He frowned down at Althea. "What seems to be wrong?"

"I feel sick to my stomach."

Ronald frowned in displeasure. The news put a damper upon his plans for the evening. "Do you want an aspirin?"

"No."

Ronald lay down beside her. Five minutes passed. Ronald raised on an elbow and began to fondle her. So she wasn't feeling up to snuff. A bit of excitement would take her mind off her troubles.

Althea began to make retching sounds; Ronald hastily drew aside. Althea tottered to the toilet and raising the seat stood over the bowl with her two hands resting on the toilet lid. Ronald fastidiously turned his back.

With the utmost care Althea lifted the lid, wedging her fingers under each end. She made more sick noises and looked cautiously toward Ronald. He lay on the couch with his back turned. She lifted the lid high, and took two long steps toward the cot. Ronald turned up a startled glance in time to see the descending porcelain lid and Althea's intent face. Ronald croaked, jerked away his head. The lid struck down with a terrible impact on Ronald's twisted shoulder; it bounced across his neck and the back of his head. He had never felt such pain before! And blood! Look at the blood! And look at the murderous she-devil who had hurt him so terribly and who now stood aghast at her failure to kill him. Ronald lurched forward. Althea opened her mouth to scream, but Ronald swept her legs out from under her and brought her to the floor; her only sound was a gasping squeak as the breath was knocked from her. She fought; she pulled his hair; she opened her mouth to scream, but Ronald knew a very effective method to prevent such betrayal.

Chapter XVII

On Wednesday morning Ben and Marcia insisted that Ellen return to school. "I know that you feel self-conscious with the pictures in the paper," said Marcia, "but it can't be helped."

"I suppose not," said Ellen glumly. "I still don't like it. Everybody will be staring at me and whispering and wondering what goes on at our house. I'll feel like a leper."

"I'm sorry, dear. It's something we've got to put up with."

"You'll find out who your friends are," said Ben drily.

Ellen shrugged. "I can stand it. But somebody should be home in case there's a call."

"I'll be home," said Marcia. "I'm not going back to work for a while. Not until we get some news."

So Ellen went to school and bore the surreptitious scrutiny with as much composure as she could summon.

Duane Mathews met her after school, and they walked to Curley's for a strawberry sundae. Duane, never voluble, seemed quieter than ever. Ellen, preoccupied with her own troubles, at last took note. "You're gloomy today!"

Duane reflected. "I suppose I am." After a moment he explained. "I don't know if you've ever noticed, but life seems to go in stages. One stage arrives and the stage before is gone, and never returns."

Ellen nodded. "I've thought of that."

"I got a letter this morning. San Jose State is taking me in January. They've got the best criminology department in the state."

Ellen stirred the spoon around in her dish.

Duane went on. "I'd like you to come with me. I want to marry you.

In fact I love you, and I can't imagine living the rest of my life without you."

Ellen smiled and tilted her head to the side. "I don't want to get married, Duane. Not right away. Maybe not for years."

"I know this is a terrible time to propose marriage," said Duane hurriedly, "what with all the trouble — in fact, I wasn't going to say anything, but I couldn't help it. When I leave here, this phase in my life is over, and I go into a new phase, and I want you to be part of it."

Ellen rose to her feet. "Let's go home, Duane."

They walked down the street in silence. At last Duane said, "Are you telling me no?"

"I don't know what I'm trying to say. I feel all muddled. Barbara and Althea are on my mind. If they're gone, I couldn't leave Mom and Dad alone. Not just yet... And I'm not sure I ever want to marry."

"You can't stay home forever."

"I know... What I'm trying to say is this. I love Mom and Dad, and they've given me a wonderful home. Ever since Dad got out of the army he's worked for the telephone company. We've never gone hungry or lacked for anything. Every year he gets three weeks with pay and we go to Arizona or Canada or Idaho. We've always had a nice time but I don't think I want that kind of life for myself. I don't want a nice little home and two or three children and a husband with a good job and three weeks off with pay every year, and lot of fringe benefits."

"Do you want a career of your own? Is that it?"

"No, it's not even that. I just want to do something exciting. I definitely don't want to get married and live in an apartment in San Jose while you're going to school... And I am fond of you, Duane. That's the terrible thing."

"But you're afraid I'd give you a comfortable home with a lawn and a patio for Sunday barbecues, and maybe a swimming pool."

Ellen laughed. "That's exactly right."

"Suppose I go to work for Interpol or join the Peace Corps or emigrate to an Australian sheep ranch?"

"I'd be very impressed. But I couldn't marry anyone now. Not while things are in such a state at home."

"I guess I'm just a dull dog," said Duane between his teeth. "I'd make a stupid spy. I don't want to teach the Hindus how to build outhouses. I can't stand sheep. I'm worthless."

Ellen took his arm. "You're not all that bad. You're the best friend I have. And I'm very fond of you."

Duane walked her to the front door of the house. "I've got to go pick up my car," he said. "Would you like to do something tonight — a movie maybe?"

"Not tonight, Duane. I don't want to leave Mom and Dad. The poor things — they're just lost without Babs and Althea."

Duane hesitated on the porch. Then he blurted, "I'm sorry I bothered you with all my plans and proposals at a time like this."

"It doesn't make any real difference." She kissed his cheek. "After all, you're human too." She found the key, opened the door and turned to look back at Duane who stood frowning at her. "What's the matter?"

"Isn't anyone home?"

"I guess Mom's gone to the store."

"If you don't mind, I think I'll come in with you and wait until someone comes home. I don't want you running off in search of Althea and leaving a note."

"Okay. Come in. You can help me with my math."

Ronald stood with his eye to the peephole. Detestable Duane and Ellen sat on the couch, Ellen with one leg tucked underneath her and a book on her lap. Ronald appraised her with the keen-eyed discrimination of an expert, trying to gauge her special characteristics. No doubt she'd be like Barbara and Althea in general, and very different in particular. Like Neapolitan ice cream: three flavors. Today his interest was purely theoretical; he was most dreadfully tired and his head and shoulder ached like sin. He hated pain more than anything; in the old days even the most trivial scrapes made him hop and palpitate, but usually his mother had been on hand to soothe him. Now the pain just wouldn't go away; any sudden motion made his head throb dreadfully.

Duane and Ellen talked in low voices: Ronald couldn't make out what they were saying. For a while he watched, then gave a sour grunt and went to lie on his cot, lowering himself with great delicacy.

Marcia Wood came home, then Ben, and Duane went away.

Ronald was in such a gruff mood that he did not even get up to see what the family ate for dinner. Their voices were quieter than usual; once Mrs. Wood said something to disturb Ellen, who spoke rather emphatically in response.

"...he did nothing of the sort!" declared Ellen. "I had a small piece and so did Duane. He doesn't like desserts all that much."

"Hmmf," said Mrs. Wood skeptically. "There wasn't much left this morning."

"Well, don't blame it on Duane. He'd be horrified if he heard what you said."

"He's not likely to hear, because I wouldn't say it to him. Anyway, I like Duane. He's a good-hearted, dependable boy, and you could do a lot worse."

"I expect I could," said Ellen. "I'm afraid that someday I might."

"I don't understand you," said Marcia.

"Today he asked me to marry him."

"My word," said Ben, "marriage at your age? You're not even out of high school."

"I told him no," said Ellen. "I'm afraid I hurt his feelings."

"The idea is ridiculous," snapped Marcia. "Duane is a nice boy, and very responsible for his age —"

"Too damn responsible," Ellen muttered.

"— but you've got college ahead of you."

Ellen changed the subject. "I suppose there's no response from the pictures?"

"Nothing the police take very seriously." Ben spoke in a forlorn voice. With a heavy heart Ellen noticed the changes which the events of the last month had worked in her father. He seemed gaunt and angular, and his skin had taken on a gray undertone. Oh why had they ever moved away from Los Gatos where life had been so easy and happy?

Ben seemed to be thinking along the same lines. "There's going to be an opening in Santa Rosa for my classification, and I'm in line for the job if I want it. We'd have to move again," he added apologetically, "which is hard on all of us."

"I'd just as soon move," said Ellen. "Whatever work we've put into this house has added to its value."

"That's for sure," said Ben, but his voice was lackluster and seemed to trail away.

Marcia clamped her jaw and her eyes glittered. "I don't particularly like Oakmead, and this house has never really been a home for us. But I hate to let it defeat us. I hate to give up and run away."

Ellen looked up in wonder. She never had suspected such complicated eddies of emotion in her nice cheerful mother. She said, "I know what you mean — at least I think I do. But is it worth the trouble?"

"I don't know," said Marcia. "But sometimes when I think of what's happened to us, for no reason at all, I just fall into a black rage." She gave a bitter laugh. "I suppose it's foolish to blame the house, but I can't help it. I do it instinctively."

Ben said uncertainly, "Well, it's something to think about anyway. Naturally we can't do much until we get our girls back, or until... well..." His voice dwindled.

"The police haven't any ideas at all?"

"Apparently not."

A week passed. The days were too long and too lonesome; Marcia finally decided to go back to work. On Tuesday Ellen came home to a quiet house. There was a peculiar rancid odor in the air, which aroused her repugnance; she left the door open and opened the living-room windows for ventilation. She started to go into the kitchen to get herself a glass of milk and an apple when the telephone rang. Ellen's best friend at school, Mary Maginnis, was at the other end, and the two talked half an hour. Ellen finally hung up and sat musing on the couch. She disliked being alone in the house; it seemed to creak and sigh and give off the most sinister noises. Ellen remembered how Althea had seriously postulated the existence of ghosts. Well, it just might be.

Ronald watched through the peephole. His aches had subsided, though for several days he had been very uncomfortable indeed. Like everyone else he found the house over-quiet with the two younger girls gone.

Nonetheless he was pleased when Marcia went back to work, and left him the privacy of the house.

Ellen had now become the focus of his interest. He had always marveled at her limpid beauty. She lacked Barbara's antic exuberance and Althea's fairy-world charm, but the peculiar luminosity was hers alone. She had commended herself to him most notably by refusing to marry Duane Mathews. Ronald would have felt savagely hurt if Ellen had done otherwise. He was also rather irritated to hear the family discussing a move to Santa Rosa, to leave him behind, lonely and remote, in his lair. There was no escaping the fact that the association he had enjoyed with the Woods was coming to an end. How wonderful if by some magic he could start all over again! In a sense Barbara and Althea were to blame for the present situation; if only they had met him on his own terms, if they had loved him as fervently as he planned they should! Instead Barbara had tried to deceive him and Althea had hurt him dreadfully, and the subsequent events were nothing but simple justice... He watched Ellen carefully, recalling how Barbara not too long ago had sat telephoning on that selfsame couch, wearing far fewer clothes. He pictured Ellen in a similar costume and the image was fascinating. Ronald considered. Should he chance another foray?... While she spoke into the telephone the project was not feasible. The time was also late; in a very few minutes one or another of the parents would be returning, and Ronald needed at least half an hour, no matter how efficiently he worked.

The next day Duane again met Ellen after school and took her in his car to Burnham's Creamery, the fanciest ice-cream parlor in town. Today Duane seemed lighter and easier. He had brooded long upon his relationship with Ellen and had recognized wherein lay his lack: he was insufficiently dashing and romantic. He was only good, gruff, earnest, responsible Duane, who eventually would make someone a good husband.

Ellen was thinking along similar lines. If only Duane could manage to be more impractical; if only he wanted to take her on a sailboat to Tahiti or a Landrover to India... Even then, she wasn't sure. Duane never quite thrilled her; he never aroused that delicious spark of primeval female wariness; he was too chivalrous and trustworthy. What a shame that Duane must be penalized for his virtues! And Ellen almost cruelly began to use several of Barbara's flirtatious tricks. And Duane thought that maybe the world was a good place after all.

Ellen said, "Daddy is talking about transferring to Santa Rosa, so maybe we'll be moving from Oakmead. Not right away, of course. We'd stay until we had news one way or another of Babs and Althea."

Duane gave his head a pessimistic shake. "That might be a long time."

Ellen reflected a moment. "I worry about Daddy. He looks terrible, all thin and gray, as if he were sick. He's anxious every minute and keeps it all bottled up inside himself. Mom — she's changing too — just how it's hard to explain. She said something strange the other night, that she didn't want to move and let the house defeat her."

Duane nodded his comprehension. "She hates the house."

"I do too," said Ellen, "but I want to move. You can't defeat a house. Nothing can bring back the old times."

"Remember how dreary it was when you first moved in? For a while it seemed cheerful — but now it's dreary again, in spite of the fresh paint."

"Last summer was fun, but even then we began to have strange notions. Remember how Althea would talk about ghosts and curses?"

"I remember very well. You never took her seriously."

"I do now. It's like there's something shadowy that moves out of sight just when you turn your head: a ghoul or a vampire who plays wicked tricks and steals food and leaves a horrid smell in the house when no one's there."

Duane raised his eyebrows. "Steals food, you say?"

Ellen reflected a moment. "Do you know, I never worried too much about it. I always thought that Mother was forgetful or that Daddy had a late snack, or that Barbara had fed one of her gluttonous cronies — but remember the other night when Mom brought home that coconut cream pie?"

Duane nodded.

"We all had a piece, and half a pie was left. The next morning there was only a quarter of a pie. Mom thought you'd taken it."

"What?" cried the scandalized Duane. "Me? I never did anything of the sort!"

"That's what I told her. I don't think it registered on Mom or Dad. They just brood about — you know what."

"And they still think I'm a pie-stealer."

"Oh no! It's just that when Mom misses something she thinks you've eaten it. It's not that she minds."

Duane rubbed his chin. "How long have you been missing things?"

"Let me think... Almost from the first. Mother is always declaring that she can't keep milk in the house."

"Hmm. Is anything else ever missing?"

"Nothing I know of. My perfume got spilled. And Althea's diary was broken open. Golly, Duane, maybe there really is something there!"

"Have you ever set a trap?"

Ellen shook her head. "No one ever took the matter seriously."

"Do you ever hear anything? Raps, bumps, footsteps, ghost noises?"

"Any old house makes noises. I've never heard footsteps." Ellen frowned. "Or did I? I hardly remember. Just the other day — but I'm not sure. The timbers creak. One night Mom and Dad heard a scream — in fact, they thought it was Babs."

"Indeed. Where did the scream come from?"

"I don't think they noticed. They looked in the street and checked me and Althea. It might have been a cat. But they swore it sounded like Babs."

"This was after Babs went away?"

"Yes. Two or three days, or thereabouts."

"Strange! They both heard it?"

"Both of them."

"Did they tell the police?"

Ellen shook her head. "There really wasn't anything to tell."

"Very very odd," muttered Duane. "Don't forget the paper those notes were written on."

"But Duane — what could it mean?"

"It means something pretty awful, that's my opinion. Let's try an experiment."

"What?" Ellen spoke in a hushed voice. "Oh, Duane, now I'm scared."

"For good reason. Listen now. Don't tell your parents, but tonight after they've gone to bed sprinkle the kitchen floor with talcum, or better, flour which won't leave an odor. Then tomorrow morning get up early, before your father and mother. What time would that be?"

"Seven-thirty. But tomorrow's Saturday. It might be later: eight or eight-thirty."

"Then you get up at seven. Go down to the kitchen, look around and call me right away. I'll get up at seven and sit by the phone. Okay?"

Ellen made a nervous grimace. "I'll do it. But what do you think we'll find?"

"I don't know, but if there *is* anything, we'll find it."

"Duane, I'm scared!"

"I am too. Above all, don't stay alone in the house. That's when Barbara and Althea disappeared — when they were home alone."

"Oh, Duane. It's really awful."

"Yes, indeed."

"Don't you think we should tell Daddy what we're doing?"

Duane shook his head. "I like your father, but sometimes he's a bit impractical."

"I know," said Ellen wanly. "He dithers a bit. He's not very aggressive. I'm not either. I'm a coward."

"But you'll sprinkle the flour? And call me tomorrow morning early?"

"Yes. I'll do that."

Duane was awake at six o'clock. He dressed, made coffee and toast, and went to sit by the telephone. Time dragged past, minute after sluggish minute. Duane sat looking at the telephone, ready to snatch it at the first vibration of sound.

At four minutes to seven the bell sounded. Duane put the receiver to his ear. "Hello?"

"Duane, it's me."

"What did you find?"

"Come over right away. As fast as you can."

"I'll be there in three minutes. Maybe less."

Duane halted in front of the house, switched off the engine, jumped to the ground. On the porch stood Ellen, in white pajamas and a blue bathrobe. Her face was pale, her eyes were wide and bright. She came forward to meet Duane. He joined her on the porch. "Did you find anything?"

"Yes, tracks! Big footprints!" She spoke in a whisper. "I was afraid to tell you over the phone. They lead from the pantry into the kitchen, then back to the pantry again. They don't go to any of the doors! It's eerie!"

"Did you look into the pantry?"

Ellen shook her head. "But there's nothing there — no place to hide: just pantry! How could anyone get into the kitchen without making tracks?"

"I don't know. Let's go look."

They went into the house, through the dining room to stand at the door into the kitchen. Ellen pointed and opened her mouth to speak, but Duane signaled her to silence. A white film covered the floor and the tracks were plain to see. They apparently had been made by large feet in slippers or scuffs, and led from the pantry to the refrigerator, where they made an incomprehensible clutter, then returned into the pantry.

"Make some coffee," said Duane in a matter-of-fact voice. But he made another sign for silence and indicated the floor. Then he fetched a broom from the back porch and swept the kitchen floor.

Ellen made coffee. She asked in a tentative voice, "Are you hungry? Should I scramble some eggs?"

"No thanks," said Duane. He stood contemplating the dining-room wall and its built-in sideboard. Then he went to the front hall and studied the wall opposite the front door.

Ellen brought him a cup of coffee. "What are you looking at?"

Duane made another gesture signifying caution. In a carefully casual voice he said, "You run up and get dressed. I'll wait for you in the car. If your parents are awake, if they want to know why I'm here, tell them — well, tell them that you invited me over for breakfast. But come out to the car as soon as you can."

Ellen nodded acquiescence. Duane thought that she had never looked so beautiful: pale and big-eyed in her blue bathrobe. He pulled her close and kissed her. "Duane, not now," said Ellen breathlessly, and ran upstairs. But as she dressed she still tingled; for almost the first time she had responded to Duane. Grim and practical Duane might be, but he was a man, and when he had kissed her he felt hard and aggressive, by no means a dull dog... She paused to listen at the door to her parents' bedroom but they were not yet astir. Ellen ran back downstairs and out to where Duane stood leaning against his car. A change had come over him; he projected purpose, a peculiar sardonic exultation; it was as if she were meeting a new person.

Duane said, "I know what's been happening." He glanced toward the house, his green eyes gleaming, then looked back to Ellen. "Do you know?"

"Well—yes. I think I do. There must be a trapdoor in the pantry, and somebody uses it to get into our house."

Duane shook his head. "It's better than that—or worse, I should say. What's on the other side of the pantry?"

Ellen frowned. "The outside porch."

"I mean on the other side."

"The living room? The stairs?"

"The stairs, and the space under the stairs."

Ellen blinked and considered. "It's all closed off," she said dubiously.

Duane nodded. "But there's somebody in there, living at the center of the house, like a worm in an apple. And I know who it is."

"Who?" asked Ellen in a faint sick voice.

"Ronald Wilby. Who else? After he murdered Carol he disappeared into thin air. The police never found hide nor hair of him. For a good reason. His mother boxed him in. There must have been a space under the stairs, a closet."

"Or a bathroom."

"Of course! The downstairs bathroom! That's where Ronald's been hiding all this time. And somehow he's able to crawl out into the pantry."

Ellen looked with horrified eyes at the house. Emotion blurred her vision; the house shimmered and pulsed like a stranded jellyfish. "How awful... But it's true, I know it's true! And Babs, and Althea... Oh my God, Duane, how utterly awful. What's happened to them?"

Duane took Ellen by the shoulders. "There's not very much doubt about what's happened to them."

"They're dead…Oh Duane." Her legs felt weak; she crumpled sobbing against Duane's chest. "My poor little sisters."

Mrs. Schumacher, coming forth to get an early start on the sprinkling, glanced at them in sniff-nosed disapproval and pointedly looked the other way. Duane and Ellen ignored her.

Ellen became quiet. After a moment she said, "How can we tell my father and mother? They're still hoping that the girls ran away to Berkeley."

"I guess we just plain tell them. There's no other way…I'd almost rather handle the situation myself."

Ellen drew back a little. "What do you mean, Duane?"

"I mean the police will come and take Ronald away and put him in a nice comfortable institution. In three or four years they'll decide he's as good as new and turn him loose." Duane stared glitter-eyed toward the house. "Myself, I'd like to kill him."

Ellen was awed by the ferocity in Duane's voice. She shuddered. "I couldn't bear to touch him, or even look at him."

"You were probably next on the list."

"Oh Duane." Ellen's breath came shallow and fast as her diaphragm jerked. "I'd go into convulsions…"

"All this time," Duane muttered. "Right under our noses."

They considered the house. Ellen asked in a hushed voice, "Do you think there's any chance that either Babs or Althea is still alive?"

"It seems awful damn remote. There's something I'd better do. You go into the house, cook breakfast, wash some dishes, just keep busy in the kitchen. And turn on the radio in there."

"And what are you going to do?"

"First I'm going to look under the house. Then I want to make sure he can't get away."

"Duane, be careful! He might harm you!"

"There's not much chance of that. In fact, none at all."

Ellen looked dubiously toward the house. "I feel all quivery inside."

"Just act natural. Don't pay any attention to the secret room. If your folks come down try to be casual."

"All right, Duane, I'll try…And please be careful, because I love you too."

Ellen went into the house. Duane took a flashlight from the glove compartment of his car and walked around to the back of the house. From inside came the thump of a cowboy band; Ellen had turned on the kitchen radio.

Duane went to the lattice-work door which opened upon the space under the house. He pulled it gingerly open and dropped to his knees. The opening exhaled a dank sour reek. Duane's nostrils twitched. He shone the flashlight here and there, but with daylight at his back the moth-pale flicker revealed nothing.

Duane drew a deep breath and crawled forward into the dark.

After ten feet he halted and again shone the flashlight around. Details of the substructure were now visible. Duane calculated that he was under the kitchen. To his right a line of piers held up a central girder which supported the floor joists. A foot over his head glinted copper water pipes and a three-inch cast-iron soil pipe. Duane traced the course of the soil pipe. Immediately beside the central girder it joined the main four-inch line from the second floor. Duane crawled to this junction and saw another three-inch soil pipe, coming down from the floor about four feet from the junction. Ronald's hiding place was for a fact the downstairs bathroom. If Ben Wood had ever entered the crawl-space, he had not been curious about his plumbing.

Duane shone the flashlight up at the floor and immediately noticed the trapdoor. He nodded somberly: about as he expected.

His eyes had adapted to the darkness. He crawled to the line of piers and shone his light around the far half of the area. Against the far wall ranged a row of brown paper sacks. One had fallen over, to spill a half-dozen tin cans carefully crushed flat. Here was Ronald's garbage dump, from which issued a stale sour-sweet odor. Duane played the light over the surface of the ground, foot by foot. There: an oblong area with a texture different to that of the surrounding soil, and not too far away another such rectangle of disturbed soil. Duane backed away. Then he halted and stared at the two areas. Someone had to find out. He crawled across the ground and with one of the flattened tin cans scraped into the loose dirt. No need to dig far. Six inches under the surface the tin can encountered something softly solid. Duane turned the flashlight down, though a waft of odor made visual inspection unnecessary. Duane nevertheless made sure.

He refilled the hole he had dug and checked the other oblong area with similar results. With stomach twitching and heart pounding, Duane covered the second hole and returned to the entrance.

He walked around the house. The lattice-work door was the single opening into the crawl-space.

At the back of the lot he found a short two-by-four, which he wedged between the edge of the concrete walk and the lattice door. Ronald's escape route was now blocked off.

Duane replaced the flashlight in his car, and went slowly back to the house. Ellen stood in the doorway. She looked at him questioningly. Duane nodded. "They're down there. Both dead, both buried."

Ellen sighed, and swallowed hard. Nothing now could shock her. Barbara and Althea. Her eyes grew dim. She felt Duane's arms around her and his voice in her ear. "I've got him locked in. He had a trapdoor into the crawl-space."

Ellen sat down on the steps. Duane sat down beside her. "My darling sisters," whispered Ellen. "I loved them so. They're gone, and I'll never see them again."

Duane put his arm around her and they sat quietly for a period. Down the stairs came Marcia Wood, followed by Ben Wood, more gray and haggard than ever.

Duane and Ellen rose to their feet. Duane went to the doorway. "Good morning."

"Good morning, Duane," said Ben Wood.

Marcia stood stiffly, looking back and forth between Duane and Ellen. "What's wrong?"

Duane said, "I wonder if you and Mr. Wood would step out here for a minute."

Ben and Marcia came slowly out on the porch. "You've had news?"

Duane nodded somberly. "Not good news."

"Oh," cried Marcia in a soft melodious voice. Ben's color became even more leaden. "Go on."

"There's no use trying to soften things," Duane muttered. "I can't make facts any better by talking around the subject. You've got to prepare yourselves for a shock."

"Go on," said Ben Wood hollowly.

"Barbara and Althea are dead. Ronald Wilby killed them."

"How do you know?" asked Marcia. Her voice had taken on a harsh, keening overtone.

"Yesterday Ellen told me about the food you've been missing. I told her to sprinkle flour on the kitchen floor. This morning we found tracks."

"Go on."

Duane paused a moment. "You know what Ronald Wilby did to my sister. Afterwards he disappeared. You know that too. Well, his mother hid him in what was then the downstairs bathroom, and he's been there ever since."

"There is no downstairs bathroom!" declared Marcia, her voice metallic.

"It's in the space under the stairs. The tracks we found led into the pantry, and nowhere else. I looked, and I could see where he'd got a way in and out under the bottom shelf."

Ben shook his head in awe. He said huskily, "This is absolutely incredible."

Marcia looked toward the house. "How do you know my girls are dead?"

"I looked under the house." Duane licked his lips. "I found Ronald's trapdoor and I found two graves. That's where they are."

Ben was like a statue carved of oak. Marcia breathed hard through her nose.

Ben finally stirred. "Can he get away?"

"Not by his trapdoor. I've wedged the outside door shut."

"Very well then," said Ben. "We'll go on in the house. I want to look the situation over. Then I'll call the police. You're sure of all this?"

"Yes, Mr. Wood. Absolutely sure."

Marcia spoke to Duane. "You saw the graves?"

"Yes."

"You're certain the girls are there?"

"I'm certain. I dug down until I found them."

Ben lurched droop-shouldered toward the house. Marcia followed, walking like a somnambulist. Ben halted in the front hall and stood staring at the wall. Marcia went through the dining room, into the kitchen and out upon the back porch.

Ben turned to Ellen and Duane. "It's beyond belief," he muttered. "All this time…"

Duane signaled him to caution. Ben sighed and nodded. "Ellen, get that number for me."

On the back porch Marcia poured a gallon of white gasoline into a basin. She carried it into the pantry and set it on a shelf, then went back into the kitchen for a paper towel, which she brought into the pantry. She dipped it into the gasoline and set it aside. Then she kicked at the secret door — once, twice, three times. The latch broke, the door burst inward. Marcia flung the gasoline through the opening. She struck a match, lit the gasoline-drenched paper towel and tossed it through: into the secret lair, into the land of Atranta, and all that magic world, with all its brave castles and evil dukes, its glorious map, and immemorial legends, became a seethe of flame. From within came a fearful scream. The sound startled Ben and Duane and Ellen, already dialing the telephone. Marcia stood in the kitchen, her face stern and calm. In the front hall the wall burst asunder; Ronald stood in the opening, blazing like a fire-demon. The three caught an instant impression of a burly figure dressed in tatters, hair and beard burning and smoking; then Ronald sprang through the front door, out into the open air. He lumbered down the steps, ran back and forth across the yard, flapping his arms, performing the most grotesque capers imaginable. He hurled himself to the ground, pounded at the flames, rolled over and over, bawling and yelling. On the porch stood Marcia and Ben: Marcia impassive, Ben slack-mouthed in wonder at this miraculous creature they had exorcised from their house. Ellen went to the telephone and called the fire department.

Ronald bounded across to the Schumacher's lawn and wallowed in the sprinkler, exuding a rancid steam. Then, as if struck by a sudden thought, he jumped to his feet and started to run. Duane tackled him and threw him to the lawn, then kicked him in the belly and cursed him. Ronald grabbed the hose and swung the sprinkler at Duane like a bolo and knocked him backwards into the Schumacher's privet hedge; then he ran off down Orchard Street and into Honeysuckle Lane.

Sirens howled; a police car appeared, followed by a fire engine. Duane halted the police car, pointed down Honeysuckle Lane, where Ronald could be seen tumbling over the fence into the grounds of the Hastings estate.

The police invaded the dank old garden, probed the thickets, searched the sheds and carriage house, scanned the upper branches of the oaks, cypresses, weeping willows, elms, cedars, and Monterey pines, but Ronald was nowhere to be found.

Five more men, the entire staff of the Oakmead Police Department, arrived to facilitate the search. Inquiries were made at neighborhood houses; pedestrians and passersby were questioned. Among the latter was Laurel Hansen, out walking Ignatz, her new poodle puppy. Laurel hastened home and communicated the news to her mother, just returning from the grocery store.

"That's just around the corner!" cried Mrs. Hansen, peering up and down the street. Hurriedly she loaded Laurel with groceries, took the remaining two bags, kicked at Ignatz who persisted in running underfoot, and trotted into the house. "Lock the patio door and the kitchen door too!" she told Laurel. "Check the windows! We're not stirring out of this house until your father gets home."

Laurel obeyed, then rejoined her mother in the kitchen. Mrs. Hansen was at the telephone, insisting that her husband come home "...actually right here in the neighborhood! Yes, Ronald Wilby!...Naturally I've locked the doors...No, Ralph, I want you to come home. Laurel and I are here alone...What could he do? He could break in and murder us both! That's what he could do!...I think that's absolutely beastly of you!...Not as soon as you can. I want you home now!...I'm absolutely serious, Ralph!...Very well then." Mrs. Hansen, jerking with agitation and biting her lips, went to look out the kitchen window. Usually so petite and poised and cool, Mrs. Hansen, in her fright and fury, seemed to give off an acrid blue fume, as of scorching metal.

Laurel asked diffidently, "Is Daddy coming home?"

"In his own good time. He's so damned inconsiderate. Like all men. It would serve him right if we went over to Edith's and left him to stew…Get his own damned dinner…Do something with your dog, he's crying to go outside."

Laurel asked doubtfully, "Do you think I'd better? I'd have to unlock the door."

"Well, make him stop his whimpering, or whatever he's doing."

"Here, Ignatz! Ignatz! Come in here now and behave yourself. No widdling on the rug!"

Mrs. Hansen muttered, "I still don't understand it. The Wilby boy came back to town? Or what?"

"They said something about him hiding somewhere, and that he was loose."

Mrs. Hansen shook her head. "And the very day he killed that little girl he was here, in this house…It's unbelievable."

Laurel excused herself to go to the bathroom. Mrs. Hansen telephoned her sister Edith and reported the sensational events of the day, "Yes, just down the street!…That little alley that runs behind the Hastings place. He escaped from wherever he was and…No, Laurel didn't actually see him, but it must have been touch and go. Naturally that damned Ralph just pooh-poohs. He told me to lock the doors and take a tranquilizer. One of these days…Laurel! Excuse me, Edith, that damned dog is whimpering. I guess he wants to go outside. Hold the line. Ignatz! Ignatz!" Mrs. Hansen put down the receiver, looked into the living room. She listened, and traced the sound down the hall to Laurel's room. Now why, she wondered, would Laurel lock the dog in her room?

She went into Laurel's bedroom, looked on both sides of the bed. The dog was in the wardrobe; she could hear it crying. Now why in the world would Laurel do something like that? She slid open the door and there stood Ronald, reeking of smoke and burnt flesh and sobbing with pain.

Mrs. Hansen stood frozen. Hissing and groaning, Ronald said, "Just a minute. It's all right, really…I just happened to walk in…I don't feel very well…"

On limp legs Mrs. Hansen retreated, her voice no more than a gargle. She turned and fled down the hall. Ronald blundered after her. "Wait!" he croaked. "Just a minute! Do you have some salve, or some aspirin?"

Mrs. Hansen threw open the front door, ran into the street. Laurel came out of the bathroom. "Hello, Laurel," said Ronald.

"Ronald Wilby," breathed Laurel.

Out in the street Mrs. Hansen babbled frantically to Ralph Hansen, who had decided to come home.

Ronald thought it best to leave. He lurched across the living room toward the patio. Ralph Hansen gave chase. The lock baffled Ronald; he hurled himself through the glass door. Ralph Hansen roared in outrage. He caught Ronald beside the swimming pool and punched him on the side of the head. Ronald toppled into the water. Moaning and crying, he clung to the coping, for the second time in his life an uninvited guest at the Hansen swimming pool, and here he remained until the police dragged him out and took him away.

CHAPTER XVIII

THE HOUSE AT 572 Orchard Street stood vacant. On the unkempt front lawn a sign read:

FOR SALE
Oakmead Realty Co.
890 Valley Boulevard
Calvin Roscoe • Bill Winger
Telephone: 477-5102

Winter rains washed over the house. A few days of early spring sunlight started weeds in the yard. From time to time Mr. Roscoe brought over prospects: young people, old people, couples with children, couples without, and at last one day Mr. Roscoe tacked a 'SOLD' placard over the sign.

A week later the new owners arrived and a van followed close after with their possessions. By sheerest coincidence Duane and Ellen happened to drive past. They halted to watch the new occupants move in: a husband, a wife and three children, two girls and a boy.

"The house looks different," said Duane. "With every new owner the house changes."

Ellen shook her head. "The house is the same. We've changed."

"There's a fine new downstairs bathroom," said Duane. "Of course it doesn't show from the street."

"I almost feel that I should warn them," said Ellen in a low voice.

Duane gave a humorless chuckle. "Warn them of what?"

"I don't know. I suppose it's a silly notion. Let's go on, Duane."

"The kids wonder why we're watching." Duane put his head out the window. "How do you like your new house?"

"Fine," said the oldest girl.

"Our school is only six blocks away," said the second girl. "We won't have to ride the bus."

"We've all got rooms to ourself!" declared the boy. "And we're going to build a big sun porch on the front so we can have porch swings, and maybe there'll be a second-floor balcony on top!"

"We're going to paint the outside green," said the oldest girl. "To match the eucalyptus."

"That sounds pretty," said Ellen. "Maybe we'll come by again when it's finished."

"You can come in and look around," said the second girl. "It's real pretty inside."

"No thanks," said Duane. "We've got to be going. Goodbye."

"Goodbye," said Ellen.

"Goodbye." "Goodbye." "Goodbye."

JACK VANCE was born in 1916 to a well-off California family that, as his childhood ended, fell upon hard times. As a young man he worked at a series of unsatisfying jobs before studying mining engineering, physics, journalism and English at the University of California Berkeley. Leaving school as America was going to war, he found a place as an ordinary seaman in the merchant marine. Later he worked as a rigger, surveyor, ceramicist, and carpenter before his steady production of sf, mystery novels, and short stories established him as a full-time writer.

His output over more than sixty years was prodigious and won him three Hugo Awards, a Nebula Award, a World Fantasy Award for lifetime achievement, as well as an Edgar from the Mystery Writers of America. The Science Fiction and Fantasy Writers of America named him a grandmaster and he was inducted into the Science Fiction Hall of Fame.

His works crossed genre boundaries, from dark fantasies (including the highly influential *Dying Earth* cycle of novels) to interstellar space operas, from heroic fantasy (the *Lyonesse* trilogy) to murder mysteries featuring a sheriff (the Joe Bain novels) in a rural California county. A Vance story often centered on a competent male protagonist thrust into a dangerous, evolving situation on a planet where adventure was his daily fare, or featured a young person setting out on a perilous odyssey over difficult terrain populated by entrenched, scheming enemies.

Late in his life, a world-spanning assemblage of Vance aficionados came together to return his works to their original form, restoring material cut by editors whose chief preoccupation was the page count of a pulp magazine. The result was the complete and authoritative *Vance Integral Edition* in 44 hardcover volumes. Spatterlight Press is now publishing the VIE texts as ebooks, and as print-on-demand paperbacks.

Colophon

This book was printed using Adobe Arno Pro as the primary text font, with NeutraFace used on the cover.

This title was created from the digital archive of the Vance Integral Edition, a series of 44 books produced under the aegis of the author by a worldwide group of his readers. The VIE project gratefully acknowledges the editorial guidance of Norma Vance, as well as the cooperation of the Department of Special Collections at Boston University, whose John Holbrook Vance collection has been an important source of textual evidence.

Special thanks to R.C. Lacovara, Patrick Dusoulier, Koen Vyverman, Paul Rhoads, Chuck King, Gregory Hansen, Suan Yong, and Josh Geller for their invaluable assistance preparing final versions of the source files.

Digitize: Richard Chandler, Joel Hedlund, Gan Uesli Starling, Koen Vyverman; Diff: Damien G. Jones, Suan Hsi Yong; Tech Proof: Rob Friefeld; Text Integrity: Rob Friefeld, Steve Sherman, Tim Stretton; Implement: Derek W. Benson, John McDonough; Security: Paul Rhoads; Compose: Andreas Irle; Comp Review: Christian J. Corley, Charles King, Paul Rhoads, Robin L. Rouch; Update Verify: Top Changwatchai, Rob Friefeld, Paul Rhoads, Robin L. Rouch; RTF-Diff: Charles King, Bill Schaub; Textport: Patrick Dusoulier; Proofread: Ian Allen, Robert Collins, Andrew Edlin, Rob Friefeld, David A. Kennedy, Rob Knight, Betty Mayfield, Errico Rescigno, Mike Schilling, Luk Schoonaert, Gabriel Stein

Artwork (maps based on original drawings by Jack and Norma Vance):

Paul Rhoads, Christopher Wood

Book Composition and Typesetting: Joel Anderson

Art Direction and Cover Design: Howard Kistler

Proofing: Chuck King, Steve Sherman

Jacket Blurb: John Vance

Management: John Vance, Koen Vyverman

Made in United States
Troutdale, OR
06/11/2024

20489844R00116